A Novel by S.Hafreth

AUTHOR'S NOTE

In Islam we believe in a third special of creation called the Jinn. As man was made from clay and the angels from light, the Jinn were created from fire. They were an older and mostly rebellious race, particularly due to their fire nature, but they were given guidance, the same as man; accepting it is their choice, again the same as man.

Stories of the Jinn have been interwoven into many popular tales of today. The genie from Aladdin, for example, is a "Jinni," and represents many of the aspects of the Jinn even in this story. Many of the ghost stories in real life, Muslims believe, are Jinn causing mischief. They can shapeshift, thus assuming different forms to deceive people. Mostly they mind their own business, but among the Jinnkind there are many troublemakers.

This work is purely fiction but is based on fact. Since the Jinn are part of the unseen world or the "ghaib" as we call it in Arabic, not much is known about them except what has been revealed.

Their wars, their relationships, their communications, and the way they think in this book are all fiction, based on imagination. Yes, there are good Jinns, but we almost never hear of them because they do not interfere with mankind, hence all of Ainee's and l-Barak's clans' motivations are derived from human behaviour.

This story is an attempt to introduce what we believe of the Jinn and how we protect ourselves from them, and that if you hold onto your true beliefs, after every hardship comes ease.

I hope you enjoy reading this book as much as I enjoyed writing it.

-S.H.

ACKNOWLEDGEMENTS

I would like to thank Zeneefa Zaneer, founder of iWords, who is a magnificent writer and mentor and a strong voice for people's rights, for reawakening the writer in me, instilling hope and pushing me to get my words out there. You are the one who got the ball rolling and to you I will forever be grateful.

Across the oceans in a land I have yet to visit, and a friend I have yet to meet in person, Zelda Solomons, you have proven that distance is nothing when it comes to measuring the strength of a friendship. Thank you for standing with me through thick and thin and for being the third "Musketeer" together with Zenee and I. May our bond be strong forever and beyond.

To my brother Shihaaz Nilafdeen, who knew that one day we would get past all our squabbles and finally see eye to eye and even be on the same page most of the time? Thank you for believing in me and helping push ATOF beyond her limits.

To my sister Zahra who was too young to understand what ATOF was about when I had first finished writing it. But you did help me sing the song I wrote for it and vowed one day you would love to read it. (Well, here we are!)

To Mossy and Possy who have always supported my little scribblings when growing up in Dubai. Thank you for supporting me throughout my writing journey from childhood 'till now and I would love to see your expression as you hold this book in your hands!

To my husband, Hafi, for enduring the long days and nights when I would traverse into the realm of my writing and not want to be disturbed. Thank you for always believing in me and silently pushing me forward.

To Shuaib, thank you, you always wanted to see your Mum as a published author and here we are now. You are turning 12 the same month as this book comes out. May you follow your dreams the way I have finally followed mine. I only hope it doesn't take you as long as it did me to find my groove.

Little Yusrab, you were nowhere on the horizon as ATOF came into being. But you surely made your way through soon after ATOF did! To date I am grateful you came when you did as it was a trying time and you brought great happiness into our lives just then.

To the late Irfan Hafiz who became a writer himself through his last years fighting Duchenne-Muscular Dystrophy, you were my role model, and epitome of strength and courage in the face of all your adversities. You kept on pushing me to publish my work. I only regret you are not here anymore to see ATOF as you would've wished to have seen her, but I know you would've been very proud. May you rest in peace.

To my readers who later became a part of my "iFamily," Heartiest thanks to you for giving me the courage to put each chapter out there. Your comments of enthusiasm were what egged me on and ATOF as a finished product today would not have been possible without you. You all know who you are.

To Sarah Buharie, "My sister from another Mister" as she would love to say, thank you for your faith in my writing. I know you will be just as happy as I am to hold this book in your hand.

To Talha, Tayeba and Mahwash, my oldest and "goldest" friends and well-wishers in OZ who have been with me through every step of my journey, cheering me on- words are not enough to thank you.

To Taryn, thank you for loving Yasmine and Ainee. It's hugely satisfying to hear of your characters touching someone's heart deeply!

And to Amanda and her beautiful family, for Line by Lion, in making my dream come true and restoring my faith in the publishing world again. If not for your, ATOF would be gathering dust on my desktop, so to speak Thank you for everything, Amanda and Thomas, for once, words fail me to thank you for bringing ATOF together and readying her for the outside world!

Dedicated to the Hafreth and Nilafdeen families.

A Novel by S.Hafreth

This book is a work of fiction. Names, characters, places, and incidents are the product of the author's imagination or are used fictitiously. Any resemblance to actual events, locales, or persons, living or dead, is coincidental.

A TOUCH OF FROST Copyright ©2018
Line By Lion Publications
www.linebylion.com

ISBN: 978-1-948807-05-0

Cover Illustration and Design © Thomas Lamkin Jr.
Edited by Taryn Love

All rights reserved. In accordance with the U.S. Copyright Act of 1976, the scanning, uploading, and electronic sharing of any part of this book without the permission of the author is unlawful piracy and the theft of the author's intellectual property. If you would like to use material from the book (other than for review purposes), prior written permission must be obtained by contacting the publisher. Thank you for your support of authors' rights

"Yet, they join the jinns as partners in worship with Allah, though He has created them (the jinns), and they attribute falsely without knowledge sons and daughters to Him. Be He Glorified and Exalted above (all) that they attribute to Him." (Qur'an 6:100)

CHAPTER ONE

February 1992

Tuesday
0800 hrs.

My eyes flew open and I felt a bit disoriented when I saw the pink canopy over my bed.

For a moment it synchronized with the dream I had been having.

Dark moonlit skies, towers of some Arabian castle, me flying in the air on an invisible magic carpet, laughing, always laughing.

Then as my brain woke up too, I remembered that this was my new bed that we had bought last night, and this was the first morning I was waking up in it.

"Yasmine, time for school, wake up!" my mama called out from downstairs.

I paid no heed to her as I continued staring up at the canopy and letting my mind drift on the last remaining currents of my flowing dream.

It was a beautiful recurring dream and there was a song also being sung in the background.

For the umpteenth time that week, I wasn't sure if it had been me or someone else singing, for even now as I struggled to remember the vanishing vestiges of that hauntingly sweet vision, I could not confirm if I was alone on my magic carpet or not.

"BOOHAHAHHA, rise and shine DING-DONG!" an ugly apparition burst into my room, shooting relentless jets of cold water at me from a toy water gun.

"GO AWAY, ABDALLAH!!" I screamed, shielding my face with my arms

"Aboodi, come out of there!" My mama rushed in to my defence and swatted at my dung-headed, chauvinistic, egocentric fifteen-year-old brother.

"Don't you know your sister is twelve and she needs her privacy?" My mother glared at my brother.

"OH. Yeah. She's hitting Pee-yoo-bertyy.." he burped rudely, stuck out his tongue at me and exited the room.

"Sorry honey," my mother said, brushing long, damp tendrils of chestnut coloured hair from my face.

I didn't reply, choosing to stare at my lap instead.

"So, how are the dreams coming along? Have the nightmares stopped?"

"I wouldn't call them nightmares, mama, "I replied softly, the glittering minarets of my dream still resounding sharply in my mind.

"Then how would you explain the sleepwalking and the screaming since the past month," she replied, already busy fluffing my pillows up against the headrest.

My mother was a busy woman, both physically and verbally. If she wasn't haranguing me about something or the other, she was fussing with an object near her reach. And most of the time she was busy doing both.

I reminded myself why I loved her so much, why I 'chose' to love her. It was because she loved me too. She was constantly worried about me.

I raised my head and covertly stared at her profile as she bent over the duvet, straightening it.

She was a striking woman in her late thirties. She had doe shaped green eyes, chestnut hair identical to mine, streaming down her back in a thick braid and her prominent cheekbones spoke of her strong character – the strong will that helped her stand on her own feet when Papa died in a rockslide accident three years ago.

Strangely, I didn't remember much of Papa. Constantly I searched my memory for tidbits showcasing his love and strength, but I hit a blank wall. Bam! It was almost as if my mind didn't want to venture into that forbidden terrain.

What mattered most was that Mama loved me and I loved her. We had a strong bond that could have borne the weight of six or seven large families. Now, Abdallah I couldn't care for much – he was such a selfish bigot when it came to the interest of other people, at my tender age I could see that – but I decided to love him for Mama's sake, for the sake of our special bond.

It was a typical snowy day in Sand Point, Alaska.

The population was not dense at all and we had only one school in Sand Point, even though there were five others in the Aleutians East Borough. There was about a total of a hundred and fifty students in our school, and a handful of Muslims, or maybe even less.

We were so few in number that there was no mosque and Jummah prayers were conducted at Mama's friend's place, just because their house was the biggest among the Muslim families. Also, since the husband was the wisest in the village, he had been appointed Imam of the community.

"OK, kids, have a good day," Mama sang, as she parked at the snow encrusted kerb and turned around in her seat to smile at me.

Aboodi always sat in the front seat, the pilferer. He didn't bother to kiss Mama or reply, but zoomed out of the car, slamming the door shut behind him. The brief gust of cold wind that sliced through the heated atmosphere inside, made me frown after him.

Mama was studying me, and her smile was tainted with a look of anxiety. The pink hijab she was wearing that morning accentuated the pink circles on her cheeks.

"Honey, are you all right?" she asked.

I nodded, wordlessly staring out the window. Inside my head my inner voice sobbed. It had been quiet for the last two days and just when I was getting optimistic, it always returned.

"Yasmine?"

I finally made eye contact with her, trying to hide the fact that I had a strong conscience.

"Goodbye, Mama," I whispered and kissed her warm cheek, before exiting the old blue Ford.

I didn't look back, knowing that I would only meet her ever-worried gaze.

That evening

1900 hrs.

    I was upstairs in my bedroom, doing my homework and also thinking of how the day had passed.

    I had known all the answers to the history pop quiz, won first place in the class Spelling Bee and also scored the maximum number of homeruns in baseball during PE.

    However, the rest of my class only shied away from me like I had leprosy.

    The group of girls I had hung out with ever since first grade when we had moved to Sand Point, were now strangers to me. All of a sudden, my 'friends' had been reduced to a quartet of whispering, gossiping little snobs calling me 'freak' whenever I passed them by.

    It had been this way for the past three weeks or so. I wondered what part of my inner turbulence showed on my face to make me repulsive to people.

    The vivid dreams I had been having had more of a mute rapture tagged to it, than the emotional upheaval a nightmare would cause.

    I began to wonder if my vivid imagination and strong conscience were starting to weaken my shell. Could it be so, I mused while tapping a Barbie pencil against my Math homework.

    No, I placated myself. I was a master poker face. I was strong. I would not show people I was battling against my will and slowly winning, hopefully.

That night I dreamed.

I was in my white nightgown, my hair streaming in a thick cascade down my back. I was standing on my window ledge looking around at the quiet, moonlit nightscape.

There was a serene beauty kissing the gossamer moon threads that speckled every snow-clad object in its path.

As I stood on the top of my bedroom window ledge, two stories high, looking out at the still night, a soft wind caressed my face, and strangely it didn't feel cold or uncomfortable.

I felt I could fly and take on the world – my world- and bravely lifted a foot and stretched it out in the empty silvery air, when I felt a presence beside me, hovering just beside my window.

That was when I woke up and realized I was screaming.

CHAPTER TWO

Ten minutes past Midnight

I woke up in my mother's arms, shivering in my nightgown, just in time to see my brother jerk my French windows shut.

I looked up into my mother's inverted face, my lips quivering with cold and a fear of the unknown. What had just happened?

Mama was sobbing as she stroked my face, my hair and even my eyes with her own eyes.

"What were you thinking, sweetheart?" she wept. "Why, why were you trying to jump out the window?"

I shifted my gaze to my brother. He was standing by my window, his arms folded across his chest, his eyes boring into mine suspiciously.

I slowly raised myself up from Mama's lap, trying to recall the fleeting images of a dream whispering farewell to my consciousness.

"I don't know," I said, more to myself than to anyone else.

Mama sniffed and frowned at me. "Sleep the remainder of the night with me, puppet. In the morning we'll see a doctor."

I was too exhausted to argue. In response, I rested my head against her arm and allowed her to lead me to her bedroom on the first floor.

As I went back to sleep, my mind wrestled with my subconscious to extract some fragment of the dream. But I couldn't get past only a feeling, not a vision, just a feeling of mystique and innocence and…

I fell into a dreamless sleep even as I thought about what the third feeling might have been.

❄ ❄ ❄

"No, Mama, pleaaassse no!" I protested the next morning at breakfast, shaking my head in vehemence.

Mama looked at me from across the scratched, round dining table, her face taut with concern.

"But you've been sleepwalking and screaming for a month now, child! We have to go see a doctor and put an end to all of this!"

"No kidding," Aboodi unnecessarily remarked from my right, as he voraciously dug into his cereal. "I've been losing precious hours of my beauty sleep. The girls at school don't think I'm hot anymore."

"Aboodi!" Mama snapped, her anger a notch or two higher than intended, probably because of her frazzled nerves.

"No one cares about your stupid looks, ugly," I said serenely, under my breath, as I whirled my spoon in my cereal.

Aboodi spun towards me and stuck his big, three-day stubbled face into mine and hissed. "Oh, just because you think the universe rotates around your supreme presence, don't expect to be any more special than that hole in the wall over there, midget! Just because Papa died doesn't mean…"

"ABDALLAH!" My Mama screamed. She actually screamed.

I whipped my head to stare at her in apprehension and saw anger transform her attractive features and make her look slightly bestial.

"Get out of the house. Go! I don't want to see your face right now." She yanked my stunned brother by the collar of his thick anorak and pushed him towards the back door.

Then she loped to the table in three big strides and snatched his backpack and thermos.

"Take this, and don't expect me to speak to you at all today." She growled, as she thrust the things at his chest.

"Mama but…" I just saw a glimpse of remorse and disbelief engulf his chiselled features as he stood there in the snow, before the backdoor was slammed in his face.

"Are you ready for me to give you a lift?" Mama said, after a minute had passed by. She was still standing, facing the door, her rigid back to me.

"What about Aboodi?" I asked tentatively, fearing that she might go into another tantrum again. It was strange. I couldn't ever recall seeing her getting this mad, not even at the sluggish telephone company men.

"He can walk to school," she replied, finally turning around. Her eyes were dry, and her face was impassive. "That'll teach him a lesson to not dredge up pointless memories and upset every one heartlessly."

You were the only one upset, Ma. I thought to myself. The only good thing to emerge out of the whole incident was Mama forgetting to make an appointment to see the doctor.

1000 hrs

It was PE period but because it was like minus twenty degrees and snow was starting to fall again, we played games in the heated gym.

"Okay kids," our PE teacher, Ms. Bellinski, clapped her hands to get our attention. We stopped idling around with our soccer balls or whatever equipment we were goofing around with to warm ourselves up.

"We are going to have an ice hockey match against Byron Bay School in South East Alaska at the end of the term, which is two months away. Our school has requested the assistance of famous Coach Burt Reynolds from Idaho, and he will be flying in next week to help us practice and form teams.

It is going to be the very first time our school will be hosting a tournament as such, and it is because thankfully this year we have the budget to do so.

So, those who are interested in signing up to be a part of this school's first ever championship, have a think about it and we will be sending a notice with you, so your parents can sign. In the meantime, let's continue our warm-up with some dodge ball!"

There was a chorus of "yah!"s and high fives and an undercurrent of excitement coursed through the air as kids anticipated the event that Ms Bellinski told us about.

Sand Point wasn't much of a theatrical place. Nothing happened here. That explained why everyone was so giddy with excitement at the thought of some silly rural match.

Ms Bellinski blew her whistle. "Dodge ball, people! I need two captains."

Without much consultation, two of the popular sporty kids walked out of the crowd of seventh graders; Alisa Mahn and Cliff Weiner.

They began calling out names and I watched silently as I saw the group on my side getting smaller and smaller as they enthusiastically joined either Alisa's or Cliff's team.

Finally, I was left awkwardly folding my hands across my chest, together with Fatty Patty.

Alisa and Cliff wanted neither of us in their teams.

"Er...Miss!" Alisa called out, waving her blond ponytail across her shoulder with a proud swerve of her head. "Can we just have nine players each?"

Ms. Bellinski looked up from a clipboard she was perusing.

"But there are still two kids left," she said. "Why, are they not feeling well?"

The kids snickered. Alisa smirked at me, as she rubbed her chin superiorly with her long, slender fingers.

"I'm fine, "I replied, ignoring the snorts and the stares coming from my classmates. In the midst of Alisa's group, I saw Samiya, my ex-best friend, from my group of friends, look at me strangely.

Fatty Patty belched softly as she straightened her glasses to peer at Ms Belinsky's face.

"No, Alisa," the teacher said dashing what appeared to have been the Snob Queen's dreams. "You can't let prejudice oversee your judgment. Please choose your player."

"I choose Patty!" Alisa quickly said just as Cliff also shouted "PATTY! WE WANT PATTY!"

Patty grinned, showing green teeth, apparently thrilled at the thought of being fought over.

"Alisa's team!" Ms Bellinski announced dispassionately. "Alisa was a split second faster than you Cliff,"

Cliff looked like someone had punched him in the stomach, as I slowly walked towards his team.

Keisha and Madison, also my ex friends but probably not as close to me as Samiya had been, whispered to one another while shooting nervous glances at me.

Trying to coat my throbbing heart with an emulsion of apathy, I decided to focus on the game itself and not the players.

My friends, my friends, the voice in my head continued to sob though. My friends hate me.

Shut up, I scolded myself. Don't give in and satisfy their cruel hunger.

Somewhere inside me, I continued sobbing, but I focused my external self to jump, skip and duck away from the ball as it kept flying towards me from the opposite team.

Strangely, after the first few minutes, I realized Alisa's team was aiming the ball at me time and time again!

Even though I darted out of the way sometimes in the nick of time and risked my own team members getting out, I felt that this was terribly unfair.

Unfortunately, Ms Bellinski was talking to someone, at the other side of the gym.

"Eat dirt, Freak!" Alisa snarled as she threw the ball with such force, it landed on my side of the net and ricocheted towards the ceiling.

I gasped in defiance, looking to my team members for support. But they either avoided my eyes or just curled their lips in disgust at me.

I began to feel that this was a game against me instead.

My inner voice rose to the surface, its sobs echoing infuriatingly in my ears and I felt a stab of grief pierce my heart. It was a grief more ancient and deep than what someone would feel if they were being cold shouldered. I couldn't explain it.

As the ball was returned to the other side, it was Samiya's turn to aim and hurl.

But as I locked eyes with her, panting with exertion and frustration, I saw her squirm in unease. I could tell she was not happy with her team's agreement at knocking solely me out of the court.

But when she lifted her arms to throw the ball and I saw her eyes graze mine with only a hint of sorrow, another image rushed in to overpower me.

A beautiful dying sunset...Samiya's face beside me in the approaching twilight...palm trees gently swaying in a summer breeze...glittering minarets of some Arabian castle, an army of black dogs racing down the cobbled courtyard...A large man embracing a woman whose back was to me...

PHOOEEEEEEEEEEEEEEEEE!!! A shrill whistle pierced my skull and the images receded behind my closed eyelids.

"Yasmine! Yasmine, are you all right? " I looked into the blurred face of Ms Bellinski. It took me a while to realize I had collapsed onto the gym floor and a sea of faces was looking into mine from above.

"Move away, move away, give her air!" the Gym teacher pushed the onlookers behind. Then she lifted my small body up in her athletic arms and walked swiftly out of the gym.

Passing Samiya on my way out, I woozily saw that she was staring at me with tears of fear and regret in her eyes.

CHAPTER THREE

Wednesday
1300 hrs

My mother worked as a salesperson at the AC store, also known as the Alaskan Commercial Company, which sold practically everything from groceries to electronics and motor vehicles.

Because Sand Point was home to only about a thousand people, the AC store was a nucleus for the community, drawing people and other stores to settle around it.

My mother had started working there only since my father's death since we needed a source of income to the house.

When asked repeatedly as to why she continued to stay in a city with broken memories, with nothing to live for anymore, she would always tell people that she didn't want to leave behind the fledgling Muslim community.

As it was, there were only four families including us and we were tightly knit like a group of people huddled for warmth in a cold, barren cave.

My mother managed to earn just enough to get us the bare necessities and then some, but recently she had been feeling edgy and tense about some problem at work.

"And if you call my mother in from work, she will be so upset and might even leave her job and then we'll all starve and die!" I cried emphatically.

The school nurse made a face. "You fainted in broad daylight," she grumped after checking my temperature and discovering that it was normal.

"But, I didn't eat breakfast!" I lied.

The nurse glanced sideways at Ms Bellinski. The latter seemed to be convinced that notifying my mama about my 'illness' was the way to go.

"Please?" I begged, squeezing a few deliberate tears. "She will be upset about nothing. And she has all that stress from work. I don't want to make her mad. I promise I will eat something now plus have breakfast tomorrow. A whopping one!"

Finally, the two adults came to a mutual decision that this time they would let the incident pass.

The minus point was that I had to devour a gigantic energy bar right in front of the stubborn nurse.

On top of a bowl of cereal for breakfast plus a naturally weak stomach, the energy bar made me want to throw up, right on the nurse's shoes, if that would only swipe off her mulish expression.

The rest of the day passed by without event.

My spirited class ignored me more than before, if that was even possible.

Samiya gave me the once-over when I walked into homeroom, but beyond that initial hint of concern, she also lapsed into the general network that disregarded me.

I sat down, feeling alone, rejected and desolate. After a few blank seconds of gazing sadly at the scratched school desk, I took out my history text book and turned to a random page.

The conquest of Persepolis, I read.

Under the heading there were graphic images of an ancient castle with huge turrets and a wide mottled moat underneath an impressive drawbridge.

Even as I looked, I could feel my active imagination take control of my senses, and fear palpitated in my heart. I was having way too many hallucinations and I didn't want this to continue.

But the images seemed to relentlessly pull me into them, and the strange thing was, the whole sensation was one of calm, as if an inner voice was consoling me and willing to guide me through the tour.

I gave in. I had no choice but to pray I wouldn't make a scene.

Sounds of swords clashing and horses neighing, and fire raging merged with the gentle drone of the voices in study hall.

I blinked and released my strong, dread-filled grip on reality.

The scene enlarged and grew brighter and the sounds grew stronger and more defiant with every passing second until the classroom had disappeared entirely, except for a dull comma shaped portal like thing at the back of my mind.

I knew that all I had to do was focus on the comma shaped doorway when I needed to escape, and forced myself to succumb to this current unfamiliar landscape.

But wait, was it really unfamiliar?

All around me a war was raging. A panorama dazzling with the fiery hues of wrath and artillery. It was brilliant but also very distressing.

I was up in the air, watching the carnage unfolding below, as a facet of history was being born.

It was surreal yet so familiar. I had seen this, witnessed this before, I was certain of it. I had lived it once.

With a shudder I realized I was looking at a memory.

"Miss Ebrahim!" A voice called to me.

It slithered down like a life rope from the small comma shaped portal somewhere in the northern portion of my brain.

I grasped it and let it lead me up and up and up, until I breezed right through it.

Just as smoothly and discretely as I had gone in, I also made my exit.

"Earth to Miss Ebrahim, come in!" the teacher in charge of study hall, Mr. Wallace, clicked his fingers at me.

I blinked once, twice. I was back one hundred percent in school, my bum firmly planted on the wooden chair. All that was left of my journey into Memoryville was the faint clash of sword on sword in my mind's eye, and even that didn't take too long to wink out.

"I've been up to Death's Door and back, trying to get you to zone in!" the teacher said, glaring at me. "Which world were you in?"

I looked down at my History book, glad that I had an alibi close to the truth.

"I was studying the conquest of Persepolis," I said in my soft voice.

"Ah-huh," the teacher said, stroking his chin in mock thought. "Persepolis- Ancient Iran or Persia- out of your Modern History of the United States book? Far out, must have taken a lot of your concentration huh?"

The class snickered as a whole.

I took my seat, trying not to let the tears of defeat and shame escape as I read the heading on the open page of my History Book.

There was nothing about the conquest of Persepolis. The title read instead – " Kennedy- The New Frontier."

CHAPTER FOUR

That evening
1900 hrs

Mama was making chili con carne for supper that evening, while Aboodi and I did our homework on our little round dining table.

There was friction in Mama's controlled conversation with Aboodi, and I wondered how long it would take before she would thaw completely.

"So, Mama, what do you think?" I asked her a trifle impatiently, as I saw her pour measured cups of stock into the pot.

"Mmm?" she said absently, not turning away from the stove.

"The ice hockey tournament! Remember!"

"Oh yes, dear," She had still not taken her hijab off from work, insisting on preparing our favourite dish before running through a shower.

"Keep the notice on the table and when you kids are in bed I will mull it over my cup of decaf."

"Aww, Mama," I groaned. "You always say that whenever you don't like something."

"What's there to like about it?" my brother whispered through clenched teeth and quickly turned to see if Mama had heard him.

I just glared back at him in reply.

"There," Mama said, tapping the side of the wooden spoon against the rim of the pot before shutting it with its glass lid. "Now, let's discuss your big match while we wait for the chili to simmer to perfection!"

I related to her whatever Ms Bellinski had told us, while Mama scanned the note in her hand, her brow furrowing in thought.

"Pretty please?" I begged her at the end of my tirade.

Out of the corner of my eye, I saw my brother shake his head and shut his book. He pushed his chair back and stretched up to his full height of five feet and eight inches.

"I'm gonna go into the living room and put on some TV," he said, yawning. "Can't endure another nanosecond of this baby babble. Call me when the food's done, Ma."

Grabbing his books from the table, he departed with heavy footsteps.

Mama looked up absently but didn't say a word. Her thoughts seemed to be far away from the cosy, aromatic kitchen of our little cottage.

Dinner was scrumptious, and everyone took more than one helping.

Afterwards, all of us sat down to some family TV and light, meaningless chatter in front of the warm, inviting fireplace.

Mama had showered and changed into her dressing gown, her hair wrapped up in her favourite orange towel which had faded to a dull peach.

While I was happily recounting some joke, I had read in a book earlier that week, I realized that Mama had finally thawed down to her usual, bubbly, engaging self.

She even punched Aboodi lightly on his muscular arm saying, "My, my, what a hunk you're growing up to be! Very soon you might have to start wearing a hijab or all the girls will fall over you!"

Both Mama and I laughed at the image of my burly brother in women's apparel, but Aboodi blushed a deep, noticeable pink. "Yeah, whatever!" he said lazily, flicking channels on the TV remote.

"Ok, bed time, Peach and Pear!" Mama said in a little while, and somewhere in my memory I searched and found that this was my childhood goodnight drill.

"You've not said that in a long time, Mama," I said, giving her a snuggly hug, before ascending the stairs to my bedroom.

"Well, I've had fun tonight, after a long time," she replied, winking.

"Me too Mama," I smiled back. "Ok, which one am I, Peach or Pear?" I asked her, playing my part and winking back.

"You're a watermelon, baby, grow up!" Aboodi pushed past me to huff off to his bedroom, which was on the same floor as mine.

I laughed louder than necessary, hoping to prove to Mama that I hadn't gotten rebuffed by Aboodi's remark. The last thing I wanted was for her to fly off her handle again and ruin the good evening.

It worked. She just raised her eyebrows inquisitively at me.

❄ ❄ ❄

In my bedroom, I was just dimming the nightlight, when my eyes fell on my schoolbag lying sprawled on the floor.

Pushing aside conflicting emotions, I hesitantly yet firmly knelt by my bag and began sorting through it, looking for one particular book.

"Ok, let's see whatcha got." I said to the book and for once the shrill voice in my head did not counter attack my decision. I guessed she too might have been piqued by curiosity the same way I was.

I opened the book a trifle timidly, once I was ensconced in the middle of my new Princess bed and wrapped cosily in my pink duvet.

Here goes nothing. I turned page after page until I arrived at "Kennedy – A new frontier."

My heart thudded painfully in my chest and I took deep breaths to circumvent the dizziness that was creeping over me.

But after two steady minutes of eyeballing the print, nothing happened.

No pictures came to life, no clash of an empowering battle could be heard, no sounds of whinnying protests…

I gave up when, after five minutes of staring at the late President Kennedy's face, the only record-breaking thing that happened was me not blinking for the longest period in my life.

Disgust laced with relief enveloped my sleepy mind and I flung the book away from the bed.

It landed with a thud under my window and I turned off the nightlight and went to sleep, feeling angry that I could not make the hallucinations come to me at a time when I was least likely to get embarrassed in public.

I closed my eyes and drifted off to sleep.

I was awakened by the sounds of aggressive combat.

All around me a war raged on and I couldn't make out who the two sides were, and I wondered how the warriors themselves knew whom to attack.

It was late afternoon and the golden light of the setting sun was tainted with the glow of bloodshed.

The castle of Persepolis was under siege.

Cannons flared, arrows flew, glinting in the numb light of the watching sun and the castle battlement quivered with the weight of it all.

I watched the whole scene with tears in my eyes.

I wasn't too high up in the air, and the warriors fighting below could have seen me clearly if they were to look up, but somewhere deeply imprinted in my very being was the knowledge that I was invisible to their eyes.

"This is murder!" someone of my rank laughed, and I turned my head and saw legion after legion of my race glide towards me, the sun at their backs.

"Welcome, Zeenon." Another voice said, its deep tones reverberating in the warm, tense air.

I looked sharply to my left and saw another group of my kind, in an army of their own, soar towards me.

Both groups advanced until they were separated only by my presence in the middle.

"*Salam*," said the tall, young and handsome leader in the front of what looked like a thousand followers from every nation and tribe around the world.

I thought he was addressing me but the leader from my pack on the right spoke up.

"Peace?" he laughed rudely. "Does the scene below look like peace to you, you mongrel!"

The first leader looked sadly at the fighting armies below.

"Well, Zeenon, I hate to point fingers but I'm afraid this war is of your making. Allah had forbidden our kind to intermingle with their kind, but you violated the covenant our ancestors made.

"You tricked those people below as well as several others around the world. And now you've let one of your women marry the king of the nation below and that is only the beginning of all the trouble. Explain yourself. Who's the nasty mongrel now?"

My heart was beating wildly in my chest as I looked at the broad chested, wise-looking leader of the rival clan.

Behind him, his host of male followers looked at us warily, their eyes ever alert, ever suspicious of us.

Then I turned towards Zeenon, a bearded, gnarly, imposing giant of a leader, and wondered how the youth of the opposing clan stood a chance against my group. We had twice the army of what they had and the females in our clan looked equally ruthless and even more determined than the stalwart men in either clan.

"You speak rubbish, Al Barak." Zeenon said maliciously. "What we choose to do, we do. The people worship us and all because of our strength and power. We are mighty!"

"And who made you mighty? Who gave you strength and power?" Al Barak, the noble opposing leader asked. "One day you'll have to return to Him and then where will your might and strength go? It'll all crumble before the One."

Zeenon smirked. "The Lord you speak of – why did he shower us with such power and influence if He didn't like us? You are nothing but a weakling Al Barak! You lead only the poor, the weak. You are afraid to think outside the box."

Al Barak did not react. He merely said, "Take away your female from the humans before it's too late! They don't even know why they are fighting one another. Stop this bloodshed now!"

Zeenon threw back his head and laughed. "Well, well. If you want us to stop this fight, then there's only one thing to do!"

He gave a signal to his army behind him. With a triumphant war cry, every man and woman shot down to the earth below, and even as they were speeding towards the drawbridge where the human massacre was continuing, I saw them change shape.

AL Barak hissed in anger as he helplessly watched Zeenon's army transform into ferocious black dogs.

A thin shimmer of light coursed through them, like a veil was being lifted from their bodies, and suddenly the humans from both sides of the battlement realized one army now had the upper hand with superhuman dogs to help them in their battle.

"Is this how you choose to end it?" Al Barak asked in a tone that was dangerously soft.

Zeenon laughed in glee as his 'dogs' dodged every arrow, sword thrust or repellent from the opposing army, and aimed for the jugular vein.

I couldn't bear to watch any further. I turned away, weighed by the unfairness of it all.

Al Barak seemed to echo my sentiments.

"Then you leave us with no choice," he said, holding his hand up high and flicking his fingers.

The effect sent a ripple running through his soldiers and as one, they opened their mouths and began to recite.

"*Bismillhir Rahmanir Raheem...*" their voices were one tidal wave of outstanding beauty, so pure and refined, it crashed into me and choked my soul.

Gasping for breath I writhed in excruciating agony and from the corner of my eyes I could see Zeenon squirm and spasm too.

"*Alif laam meem...*"

Stop, stopppppp, my eardrums seemed to be throbbing and pulsating, on the verge of exploding.

My throat felt constricted.

My eyes rolled back into my head.

Their incantation was so melodious, so powerfully sweet and yet so lethal.

The essence of what they were chanting was mercilessly threatening to cleave me down the middle.

I needed to get out of here. I needed to escape. I needed to do it now.

"Yasmine! Yasmine!"

I was screaming and screaming.

Then I threw up all over myself.

And screamed some more.

"YASMINE!"

I screamed and screamed, my eyes were pinched shut and I screamed like no one could hear me and I could hear no one.

"YASMINE, STOP IT!"

A sudden sharp crack and a powerful sting on my cheek sent me keeling over.

That was when I opened my eyes and started crying uncontrollably.

"YASMINE!" My mother's voice. My bedroom. Home.

I was back.

The realization made me cry even louder.

"I'm sorry I had to slap you," Mama was saying in the background, as I shut my eyes again and continued to sob.

I felt myself being lifted up and cuddled against a warm surface and a rapidly beating heart.

"Shh, shhhhh. Mama's here now, it was only a bad dream, only a bad dream, you are safe now, you are safe."

The next morning Mama insisted that I skip school and go with her to see the doctor.

CHAPTER FIVE

Thursday morning
1100 hrs

"Can you describe the dreams to me?" Dr Cardiff asked me gently.

After waiting for two hours in the boring lounge, we had been ushered into this elderly man's cramped office only to be asked wide-spectrum questions.

I looked up at the boring white ceiling and dangled my legs absently.

"Yasmine!" Mama snapped at me from the left. "Stop acting like a baby and answer the good doctor!"

I sighed and looked at the doctor, who was smiling patiently at me.

"Describe them, how?" I asked serenely and purposefully as I lightly tapped the heel of my left shoe against the metal leg of the chair.

My mother rolled her eyes. The doctor continued smiling passively. I wanted to fall asleep but was afraid that I would dream again. It was a total no-win situation for me.

"Can you please describe to me what you see in these dreams of yours? I want to know what mood they pertain to." he said.

The mood? I wondered. What was he asking me about? I tapped my heel faster in frustration.

"I dunno," I mumbled, staring at my lap. Mama laid a warning hand on my jerking knee and stopped my restless heel tapping.

"I guess I have different dreams every time and sometimes the dreams fade away when I wake up," I said. "Sometimes I don't remember them. Most of the time I realize . . .I am screaming in real life."

"Or sleepwalking or trying to jump out of a window," Mama added, glancing at me.

"Mama!" I protested, somehow feeling that I was slowly being stripped, with each and every detail of my life being laid out before this strange old man.

"The window incident happened only once!"

"Once is enough, Yasmine," Mama said sternly. "It's a long fall to the hard, rocky ground below. You wouldn't have survived to do a repeat." She shuddered.

The doctor scribbled fervently in a pad.

"So they are scary dreams?" he asked.

"Not always. I remember waking up feeling happy several times, but lately I think they are becoming um... a bit sinister? "

"And it's not only the dreams at night, you say?" he asked, his pen merrily scribbling away while his eyes darted between Mama and me.

"You also mentioned sudden visions in broad daylight…"

"Yes," Mama confirmed.

"Where were you when the visions occurred the last time round, Yasmine?"

I bit my lip, rolled my eyes and thought of the promised ice-cream after this long, stupid visit.

"Well, at school, during PE. We were playing dodge ball."

"And you weren't hit by the ball or anything? It was a coincidence that you just had a vision and fainted?" he asked.

I moved around in my constrained chair, my discomfort rising.

"Yes," I replied, not meeting his gaze.

"Hmm," he scribbled something else in his diary, with less ferocity than before, before looking up at us again.

"Thank you, Yasmine," he said to me. "Now, if you could please return to the waiting room, I would like to have a few words with your mother."

It was an order that I was tempted to defy, just to make the remaining hairs on his head also turn white.

But I didn't. Against my will, I stood up and walked languidly out of the office, dreading the time I would be spending in the torturously bland waiting room.

They didn't have many magazines on the coffee table and I was the only person around to notice this.

The only other source of life in this part of the building was the fat nurse behind a scratched counter, but at least she had headphones on and music to beat the boredom away.

Sighing loudly to myself, I sifted through the magazines.

Sports, sports, more sports and aah! A Woman's Weekly!

I reached out to grab the rather outdated copy, when a small voice in my head said Yuck!

I frowned and lifted the magazine anyway.

I skimmed through a cover story on the breakthrough of research indicating that folic acid reduced the cases of neural tube defects in fetuses.

Yuck, my mind scoffed.

I turned to another page where beauty tips and secrets were revealed and yet to another page where an Aunt Agony answered questions about marital problems and waxing horrors.

Yuck! Yuck! Yuck!

I put down the magazine, my own interest in perusing those articles diminishing with the burst of repugnance that was filling my senses.

I couldn't understand why one part of my brain liked something while another part rebelled against that choice.

While I was musing over this, the door to the Doctor's office burst open and my mother came storming out.

"Good day, Doctor!" she snapped and banged the door shut.

"Come on, Yasmine, we have wasted enough of our time here," she said to me and led me past the unreceptive nurse at the desk.

"What's wrong?" I asked, running behind her as she took swift strides towards our car.

"Get in the car, Yasmine, we are going home!"

"But, Mama," I argued as I clicked on my belt. "Why are you upset? What did he tell you?"

She muttered something under her breath as she started the engine and prepared to reverse out of the parking lot.

"No wonder nobody comes to this dump, it's hopeless!" she said more to herself than to me. "I should've straightaway booked an appointment at the hospital for you instead of relying on this cheap garbage close to our house."

"But..."

"Yasmine," she said, swerving onto the main road. "There is nothing wrong with you all right! You are a perfectly healthy, perfectly sane child coming from a normal, happy family. Don't let anyone else tell you otherwise!"

"Oookaaay..." I said confused. My mind latched onto the word she had just uttered: sane.

"And," she continued with resolve in her tone, "You are joining the ice-hockey team! Go and show them the stuff you're made of!"

So, ice-hockey replaced the ice-cream that I was supposed to have, and I didn't remind Mama about it either. My appetite had vamoosed.

What was now on my mind was the confirmation that there was something wrong with me and I meant to get to the bottom of it.

CHAPTER SIX

Saturday morning
0900 hrs

Ever since that futile trip to the doctor's, my strange visions and dreams had not made an appearance. Thankfully.

On Saturday morning, I woke up to the smell of something good wafting up from the kitchen.

I hastily cleaned my teeth, washed my face, brushed my stubborn chestnut locks into a haphazard ponytail and thudded downstairs.

"Good Morning, Mama!" I called out. The aroma was tantalizing.

"*Assalamu alaikum*, angel – Peace be on you," Mama turned towards me from the busy stove. She had all four burners working, plus the large oven underneath.

"Wow, are we having a feast?" I asked, wide-eyed.

"Sure we are!" she kissed the top of my head and handed me a plate with eggs and toast. "Eat up! I am making your favourite for lunch and we are also having guests over to join us."

"Mmm," I said, already stuffing my face. "Do I smell chocolate cake?"

"Yes, but that's for dessert. Now did you say '*Bismillah*' before your first bite?"

I nodded hastily, even though I hadn't started my meal with the little prayer that began most activities with God's name.

"Mama, can I have all the eggs from the pan?" I asked her a couple of minutes later. "I'm so hungry!"

"But your brother…"

"…won't wakeup till midday and by then he can have lunch!" I winked saucily at her.

"My, my!" she smiled. "Aren't we a feisty lot today? Ok, then, I see your point. Besides you must be hitting a growth spurt! That was three eggs on your plate already! But I am not complaining, it's about time you sprouted. "With that she ladled the remainder of the scrambled eggs onto my plate.

"So, who's coming today?" I asked her between mouthfuls, as she grated some Gouda over the eggs.

"Yusuf and Layla Khulood and Samiya and her folks."

Yusuf was the Imam and Layla was his wife. I didn't have any problem with them.

But the thought of Samiya coming over dampened my spirits a tad.

There was some mystery as to why she and the whole school was against me, but try as I might, I couldn't open that memory.

It was similar to the struggle I endured each time I tried to remember Papa and what happened to him. I drew a blank.

"I tried calling the Morrisons too, but they declined because they were going trekking this weekend," Mama continued. "Too bad your brother won't have Muhammed to hang around with. He might just end up at the youth club again! That boy is getting a bit too hard for me to handle…"

I was only vaguely listening to her. My brain struggled to pick the locks of the door hiding these enticing secrets, but once again I failed.

❄ ❄ ❄

The guests arrived just after noon.

First the Imam and his wife walked in, bearing wrapped gift boxes though it was nobody's birthday nor was today a function of any kind.

The Imam was a tall, heavily built, African American man with salt and pepper hair cropped close to his head and a shaggy beard that I was certain would serve as a sufficient blanket during these winter months.

He radiated an aura of terror and awe or maybe that's how I felt, because Mama smilingly greeted him and hugged his wife, while my brother shook his hands and got a hearty clap on his back.

"Assalamu alaikum, little one, my, you are growing!" he boomed in his guttural voice as he directed those piercing coal-black eyes of his into mine.

I shivered, even though the heaters were on at full blast and the front door was shut.

"Come on, don't glare at her like that!" his wife, a petite brunette with peaches and cream skin to die for, punched him lightly on the arm. "You're frightening her!"

The Imam turned to his wife in protest. "But I wasn't glaring!"

"You don't know your own strength, Bear!" she nudged him and thankfully pulled him out of the little foyer where we were grouped around, and into the warm and inviting living room.

He turned and rolled his eyes at Mama while he was being ushered out. She in turn smiled sympathetically at him, before turning to frown at me.

"Ok, Mama, I'm off to the club!" Aboodi declared and reached for the door handle before Mama could react.

Just then the doorbell chimed.

"Abdallah, listen to me young man, we have guests today!" Mama hissed as she seized him by his jacket sleeve. "For one blessed day can you not stay out of that confounded club? At the very least, stay to greet our other guests too!"

He raised an eyebrow at her, yanked his sleeve away and pulled the door open.

"Assalamu alaikum!!!" Two eager voices burst through the chilly air.

Mr. and Mrs. Mehmet and their daughter Samiya were standing on the doorstep, brandishing a big and luscious fruit basket.

Samiya was looking sulky as if she had been dragged here against her will. Also, she was wearing a beautifully embroidered scarf on her head, and as she saw me gaze curiously at her, she turned red and started scuffing her boot against the snow-coated flowerbed.

"Wa alaikumu salam!" my brother replied in a falsely cheerful voice and turned back to look pointedly at Mama before stepping out and brushing past the Mehmets.

"Come in, come in," Mama called out to the visitors in this choked voice, as I saw her follow my selfish brother's disappearing figure over the Mehmet's heads.

Once coats were hung up and everyone had greeted one another in the living room, snacks were passed out.

"Mmm…that smells refreshing!" Layla, the Imam's wife said, sniffing the air. "What's cooking, Mariam?"

"Roast turkey," Mama smiled, looking in my direction. "Yasmine's favourite."

I blushed, as all eyes turned towards me. I couldn't get over the Imam's sizzling gaze and decided I would hate the man from now on. He was such a menacing figure.

Samiya was seated in an armchair closest to the bookcase in the corner, as far away from me as she could get.

The rhinestones in her headscarf glittered and winked in the reflection from the fire blazing hungrily in the front of the room.

I decided that there was no better opportunity than now to open my locked door with the key seated in the same room as me.

Just as I opened my mouth to ask my once-friend if she would like to play some board games before lunch, her mother unknowingly broadened the gap for me by commencing a new conversation thread.

"Is that Exotic Arabian food you've made?" Mrs. Mehmet asked, walking to the kitchen counter and lifting the foil off a tray to have a peek.

My mother nodded as she served appetizers around.

"You do know *Mooghrabieh*, don't you, and *Kofte*?"

Samiya's mother nodded, looking very pleased. "It sits well with my Lebanese roots and Ahmed's adopted Turkish ones. Haven't had it for ages though. This looks and smells authentic!"

"Now don't take my comment as a racial one, Mariam," began the Imam's wife and I nervously twisted the big toe of my left foot around the right one, desperate for a moment to get Samiya's attention.

"You know that I married Yusuf after his first wife died. So, I haven't been here for too long. But tell me, you are American right. I mean you do look like a true-blue country girl and you sound like one too! That delightful southern twang!" A titter.

My mother laughed. "But I am! I guess you can take the girl outta the country but not the country outta the girl! I was born and raised in Texas. My folks still have a farm there which we go to every other Christmas. You see they are not

Muslim, but I still go to spend some time with them during the holidays."

The whole room went quiet except for the crackling of the fire and the munching of crisps and pretzels. It was as if everyone leaned in to listen to my mother's story, even though I was sure everyone except Layla knew it.

My mother however was not keen to embark on a long and sordid tale of her life. She just cut to the chase.

"Well, Layla, marrying Sa'eed opened up my eyes to a whole new world, a whole new range of ideas and beliefs. Sadly, his job led him here, into the middle of nowhere and I couldn't say no to his dream.

So we tried to stick to tradition or what's left of it. Homemade country food, pies, and in my late husband's case, a touch of Middle Easterness, because even though his family have been sprinkled all over the world for generations, his direct ancestors have always lived in Iran."

I pricked my ears. Iran. Persia. The throbbing grail in my restless dreams.

"So, from time to time, I do make exotic food, but I'm sure my children and I don't recall the last time I splurged. Living here on the outskirts of civilization has taught us to be frugal. I mean if not for the Morrisons hunting every other week and getting us all fresh meat, we would hardly have anything *halal* to eat!"

"Yeah we'd all have to survive on daily halibut and Pollock and the berries growing on our doorstep." Samiya's mother said, raising her glass.

"So why do you still stay here?" Layla tossed the famous question.

"Because as it is we're almost extinct as the Bengal Tiger, you silly puss!" the Imam growled, with a smile. "Are you asking one of our brethren to just up and leave? A nice minister's wife you make! Pah!"

Everyone broke into good natured laughter.

I looked once again at Samiya. She was half turned away, gazing dreamily into the fireplace, her face almost hidden from sight.

"So, how old are you, dear?" Layla turned towards me next, ever hungry for information.

"Twelve," I said.

Her mouth fell open. "But I thought you must be at least nine! Surely you can't be.."

"Layla!" the Imam shushed her quickly. His voice boomed majestically around the room and back, and even Samiya was jerked awake from her silent reverie.

"Girls," my mother said quietly, looking from me to Samiya. "Why don't you go to the backyard and make snow bunnies or something? It's much warmer now and before the snow melts I would like some structure in our garden please. Every other house has a snowman or two. Only ours looks like we've got an old couple living here. Now go on!"

I looked anxiously at Samiya. She looked at Mama as if she had just grounded her here for life.

"But," she began in a small, weak voice.

"No buts," intervened her mother sharply. "Just go! You two need some life in your bones. Go outside, be children, and not a couple of middle-aged aunts!"

"Yes, and please don't forget to wear your coats and mittens!" my mother said, her tone revealing that she was happy to have an ally to back her up.

Just like that my opportunity had come. I stood up from the piano seat I had been pasted to and shuffled towards the back door.

Samiya morosely followed suit.

This is it, I thought, my heart thumping wildly under my sweater. Now I might find out the solution to what appeared to be a big portion of my worries.

CHAPTER SEVEN

Saturday
1300 hrs

Our backyard was a decent size with a six-foot wooden fence jaggedly running around the perimeter.

There were a few houses, in similar structure to ours, on our right and even more so on our left.

All of their backyards had snowmen in them, each one grinning defensively like sentinels guarding each house.

Even though it hadn't snowed in a couple of days, the temperature had hardly risen, and the sun blinked weakly from the sky as it threw its pale, exhausted light around the white landscape.

I slyly looked out the corner of my eye at Samiya. She was standing abreast of me, tall and stiff, arms folded stubbornly across her chest, head turned to the right.

I cleared my throat and took a step forward to pick up a random twig half buried in the snow. "Hey, wouldn't this be a nice nose for our snowman," I asked, trying to inject a bit of jubilation into my dry, weedy voice. "I'm sure Mama would have used up all the carrots for lunch!"

Samiya didn't flinch.

I sighed. I could pull this off the easy way or the hard way.

The easy way was apparently a flop as wide as the Yukon River.

I cleared my throat again, flipped my ponytail behind my shoulder and squeezed my eyes shut, trying to think of the best way to stir up her cauldron.

Images of us laughing, swam in front of my eyes. A bubbling creek. Very late afternoon. The sound of galloping hooves. A parked car.

My heart stopped beating.

A parked blue Ford.

"Samiya!" I said, opening my eyes in a flash. Red spots clouded my vision. "Samiya? What were you and I doing on one particular night near the Hyongu Creek?"

❄ ❄ ❄

It worked.

Samiya jumped as if I had prodded her with a live wire.

She whipped her face toward me, her hands pressing her chest.

"How dare you!" she whispered, her hazel eyes dilating in fear. "How dare you bring that horrible memory up again! How could you?"

I bit my lips. The rock had shifted a bit and I could now make out a chink of light. But it was not enough.

"Samiya, listen to me," I pleaded, taking a step toward her. She quickly took three steps behind.

"Listen, something happened somewhere, sometime in my life and I...I'm lost...I need someone to refresh my memory."

She looked around her in alarm, her face turning white with every passing second.

"Samiya," I said, my voice fading against the vicious thumping of my heart. "Samiya, I need to remember. Please. I need to know what's happening. Just tell me this, is it because of THAT night that you stopped speaking to me?"

She just stared at me, barely breathing, her hands still pressed against her chest.

"Did something happen to me then? Did I do something so wicked that everyone hates me? Good heavens, Samiya! I need to know the truth! I cannot remember!"

An icy wind whipped through the stillness of the air.

Great, I thought as my cheeks turned numb. Perfect storybook moment, and still she misses her cue.

But something moved in her. She blinked, took a slow breath and licked her chapped lips.

"And here I was worried you would say something about my *hijab*," she said drily.

This was the first civil sentence she had spoken to me in ages.

It conveniently broke the ice, but I did not, could not laugh, funny and outrageously inappropriate as the comment seemed to be in the tension surrounding us.

Samiya looked down at her boots. Her breath came out in healthy white puffs of mist.

"I never thought this day would come," she whispered, her voice as soft as a snowflake falling on a leaf. "But then again I was also afraid that it would indeed come."

I tried to breathe as quietly as I could, to take in each and every word of hers in their raw, complete form.

She looked into my waiting, anxious face, her dark eyes slowly filling with tears.

"I never meant to turn away from you, Yasmine. But after that night, I was scared. What I saw frightened me. And you...you changed. Gradually you changed. You're still changing."

"What?" I whispered, feeling I would explode with the intensity of the suspense I was drenched in. But I was scared to voice my emotions lest I break the delicate, agreeable state Samiya was in.

"You are, Yasmine," she said, her eyes moving over my face and my flyaway hair under my knit cap, "Changing. That's why I became afraid of you."

"What are you talking about? I don't understand!" My voice broke through a decibel or two; I could not constrain my agony at the mounting apprehension.

"Why do you think the rest of the class avoids you?" she asked. "You were so normal before THAT night. You were average. You were you. But after that you have slowly become...Oh I dunno. You have this weird look on you face most of the time. It's like you walk around with a cloak to push people away. And then you daydream every time. Like the other day with the history book."

Pink circles stole over the pallor of her cheeks as her voice got more and more heated.

"You just creep people out, Yasmine! Then again you are…the best at games, at Math, at quizzes and surprise tests…it's like you're a machine that can never fail. You were so not like that! Like I said, you were average! But now it's like you are…you are…"

"Invulnerable," I supplied, quietly.

Samiya shook her head. "All those big words. Sometimes you act so mature like you're a grown up. At other times you're way too babyish for your age. And you haven't grown an inch since that night. It's like you're stuck in a nine-year old's body! You're all messed up inside!"

I should have reeled from the effect of her words. But a major part of me was still processing what she had said. Another part was still angry that the answers she had given did not appease the questions racing in my mind.

"But what happened?" I pressed her. "What was Mama's car doing there? What were *we* doing there?"

"I'm sorry," she said, clasping a gloved hand to her mouth and shaking her head. It seemed that the spell she had been under had lifted.

"I don't know who you are anymore Yasmine, I can't, I won't go back to that dreadful night. It was a horrible one. I wish…I have always wished I never listened to you and went with you to that ravine!"

Ravine…Tillman's Gorge.

Another door unlocked just then and creaked open beckoningly.

The rock in my head groaned and more light seeped in.

A second wind whipped through us, chilling me to the bone.

"Samiya, if you don't help me, who else will?" I begged, and I grovelled with every ounce of my being.

She stared at me, the tears freezing off her face even before they could properly slide down.

"Your Dad," she replied. "He was there too, just before he died."

CHAPTER EIGHT

Saturday
1315pm

Samiya opened the screen door and rushed inside, and I determinedly followed her.

"Don't ever talk to me again about that night, I beg you!" she turned around and hissed at me, her large eyes fearful.

"Samiya, you can't just tell me about my Dad and stop point blank! I need answers!" I argued as I closed the screen door behind me.

"You didn't bother me for nearly three years! And now you want answers?" she spat back.

"Samiya, listen!" I said, inching close to her and looking up into her flushed face.

"It's like I've woken up from a long dream or something a month or so ago...I have big patches in my memory and then I'm having these visions of things that could not have happened to me! Not in this body anyway! I want to get to the bottom of this Samiya...

"You know I can't ask my dad what happened that night because he's dead. Mama has hidden all the photos because she once said it brings her too much grief."

Samiya stared open-mouthed at me and I could almost see the wheels turning in her head.

Will she surrender to my emotional speech and tell me the truth of that night, or will stubbornness get the better of her?

Just at that moment, a peal of laughter erupted from the living room.

"I know, she was like, no way am I gonna wear that hanky on my head!" Samiya's mother could be heard saying.

"But how did you convince her to wear the *hijab*?" I heard my mama ask.

"I said, 'you wear this and there'll be no hanky panky, dear!' and she was speechless!"

"I don't believe it!" Samiya gritted her teeth as everyone laughed in the background. "There are men there! And she is making fun of me!"

"But why did she suddenly decide for you to wear it anyway?" I asked.

Samiya brushed an angry tear from her cheek. "Because I got my period yesterday, after school, that's why. And she's like, oh now you're a woman, *Samee-ah*, you'll have to dress modestly, *Samee-ah*. No more playing with boys on the streets, *Samee-ah*!"

Samiya sniffed and broke into full-fledged tears.

"I hate this; I hate whatever's happening to me. She's gonna make me wear it to school too! Everyone will laugh at me! No one will be my friend anymore!"

I was about to point out to her that this was exactly what had been happening to me for a while but didn't have the heart to stuff it in her face.

"I'll strike you a deal," I told her, as I laid an arm around her quaking shoulders. "I'll make sure no one makes fun of you at school, if you promise to go back to being my friend and help solve my mystery. Deal?"

She was sobbing too hard and trying to keep quiet at the same time. She nodded, her face a red, streaming mess.

"Ok, I'll help you." she said. "After lunch, we'll go up to your room."

❄ ❄ ❄

Throughout Mama's wonderful roast turkey and winter vegetables with its fusion of Middle-Eastern sides, the adults chatted, joked and praised the meal.

Samiya ineptly decided to either ignore her mother when she addressed her or grunt and nod instead.

At one stage her bewildered mother looked to me for an answer, but I just shrugged, hoping to kick Samiya under the table to bring her back to her senses.

Unfortunately, my legs weren't long enough.

For dessert Mama brought out the lovely chocolate cake with swirly chocolate frosting dusted with icing sugar and pecans.

"OOOOOH!" breathed everyone as they watched it being wheeled out on a little trolley.

"Mama, can Samiya and I go upstairs with our dessert plates?" I asked.

"I don't see why not, if you two girls are having so much fun!" Mama smiled back, adding, "You look beautiful in your *hijab*, Samiya, *Maasha allah*!"

"Thanks," Samiya said stiffly.

"Welcome to the club, young one!" Layla winked.

I swiftly took our saucers upstairs, afraid that if we hung out any longer with the adults, they might dampen Samiya's mood and she would go back on her promise.

We sat on my bed and began eviscerating our gooey dessert.

I waited for Samiya to say something, but for a long time, the only sound made was the clink of our forks on our plates.

"You know...I wonder why I can't remember my Dad." I began, not looking up from my half-eaten slice of cake. "It's only been three years. Not ten or so."

"Mm hmmm..." Samiya murmured unintelligibly.

"Samiya!" I couldn't take it any longer. "You promised you would help me!"

"All right, already!" she looked taken aback. "I was gonna discuss it once the cake was done."

I rolled my eyes.

"When did you get this bed?" she asked, bouncing up and down a little. "It looks new."

"It is," I said, wondering if she would be asking about the roof next.

"Why did your mama get you a new one?"

"Because the old one was falling apart, and she thought that was the reason for my nightmares."

"No kidding?" Samiya's eyes were wide.

I shook my head and gobbled down the last of my cake.

"When did the nightmares start?"

I sighed. This was the doctor's visit all over again. But if you want something, you have to give a little in return.

"I'm not sure," I said, shrugging. "Maybe a month or more. But they didn't begin as nightmares. They were more like vivid dreams that I could never remember when I was awake. It's only recently that they are becoming more corporal, if you know what I mean?"

She looked blankly at me. "No."

"Corporal," I repeated, trying to come up with an easier synonym.

"You mean like army commander?" Samiya asked, frowning.

"No," I said, sighing. "I meant now the dreams are becoming more realistic, more…dynamic, more movie-like…"

"Ah-huh," she nodded, still frowning.

"And now, they are losing their pleasant feeling when I wake up. And also, I can remember what I dream or see. And lately it's I dunno...bizarre...I can't control it... the images I see are so familiar yet it's impossible those are my own. It's like I'm seeing memories that I've forgotten or from another life I've lived previously."

Samiya bit her bottom lip and thoughtfully pricked her fork into the remaining bit of cake on her plate.

"Three years ago, after your father died, you were changed." She said, not looking up from her plate.

"It was like you went all quiet for a few months and everyone thought you were suffering from grief. Then you started to get really ill several times a month, every month and there was a time when Aunt Mariam thought you would die, you were wasting away...don't you honestly remember any of this?"

I was drinking in her words. Did I remember? How had I forgotten? I plunged deep into the vaults of my rusty memory and prodded for some image to confirm Samiya's statement.

Wisps of a memory of me lying in a bed, bathed in fever, weakly floated to the surface.

"Go on," I whispered, pinching my eyes shut and concentrating hard.

"You couldn't even make it to school for about a year," Samiya continued in her hushed voice. Then at the end of class five when everyone thought you were going to snuff out, you recovered.

"It was a miracle, my Mama said! Imam Yusuf who was never around much back then and also recently a widower, said it was a test from God and we should all be thankful for His limitless bounties.

"So, in sixth grade you returned. You were a ghost of your former self, really Yasmine. You were all shrivelled up and white and barely spoke to anybody. And half the time you were whispering to yourself, shaking your head and having minor fits.

At first we tried to help you but then you started to frighten us really. It was like you were at war with yourself…"

The voices in my head, I thought, my eyes still shut. My contradicting conscience could have easily been another person arguing with me.

"And after the Christmas holidays, when you returned, you had changed yet again." Samiya continued. "You were still daydreaming in class and not talking to us much, but then you developed this superhuman ability to succeed at everything you tried! Like I said, class tests, General Knowledge questions, sports- anything."

"It's like me, Madison, Keisha and Mikeala had never known you. Or like you had never known us. And the rest of the class, including Alisa Mahn, were appalled that a shrivelled, white little shrimp could outrun them at everything."

I opened my eyes. Samiya had prodded her cake to smithereens with her fork.

"That's what I heard Alisa say in the locker room one day," Samiya said defensively, looking up at me. "Shrivelled little shrimp – not my words!"

"So, what happened to Dad." I asked her, unflinching. "What happened that evening when something changed me, that made me forget so many important events in my life?"

An involuntary shudder ran through my friend's body. Her face contorted into a mask of dread.

"Yasmine," she pleaded, her voice drizzled with reluctance.

I laid my hand on top of hers consolingly. "I promise you, Samiya, if I could remember, I wouldn't be making you go through this torture. But I really need to know."

She exhaled in quick sharp breaths. I tightened my grip on her hand, trying to let my compassion and positive energy flow through.

"On the night of May 18th, 1989," she began, her voice cocooned with caution. "You told me that you wanted me to meet a friend of yours. It was somebody secret, you said. You had told me about her before too and asked me to not tell another living soul about her, not even Mikaela and the girls. This was the night you said you would introduce me to her."

"So, I came to your house telling Mama that I had a project that was due the next day, Friday..."

BAM! I was hit by a sharp, unanticipated vision.

I could still see my hand on top of Samiya's, in the blackening distance, whilst in the forefront, the door that had only creaked earlier burst fully open, giving birth to a vivid memory.

I was peering at a second story window from my crouched, hidden position in the shrubs nearby.

It was late afternoon, probably an hour or two before sunset.

A few birds called out to one another in the whispering trees above and I slithered towards the window where I could distinctly hear voices pour out from.

"Even though I was excited to meet your friend, I was also jealous," Samiya's voice droned on in the background. "You see, you had told me that she had extraordinary powers and I thought you might prefer her over me. I was afraid at the same time, but also curious. Very curious to meet her and see if she could do all that you told me she was able to do."

I slithered to the foot of the cottage, my forked tongue darting out to taste the tepid air.

"*Yasmine, where is she?*" I heard someone above me ask in a high-pitched girly voice.

"*She said she'll be here soon. She never breaks a promise!*" said another voice, equally excited but more controlled.

I slid my tongue out again. Something was not right, there was tension bubbling in my chest. For her sake, for the mysterious woman in the ravine, I had to get the little girl to trust me and to follow me.

And yet I didn't want to hand over the little girl to the woman. I had begun to develop a soft spot for the chestnut haired, brown eyed, bubbly little...

"I mean what scrawny, little nine-year-old wouldn't believe in magic and ghosts and fairies!" Samiya said, sniffing, her words echoing from the present. "I just had to see it though! I had to see through my own eyes, your friend changing shape, Yasmine!"

I uncoiled my long, thick, undulating body and began to focus on an image. A picture of the brown haired beautiful little girl upstairs swam in my mind and I felt my body converge on itself.

I shrunk and collapsed, then began to rise upwards, my skin slowly melting from coal-black to a beautiful, pale, translucent blue.

I stood up - a beautiful humanoid young woman with hair as black as the approaching task in my mind and floated towards the window.

"And just when I was beginning to think you had been pulling my leg, she appeared!" Samiya, from the present, said and squeezed my hand. I felt the contact as if it was a few light years away.

I drifted toward the window, as light as the caress of a summer breeze, and perched on the open windowsill.

Inside was a girl's bedroom littered with pink Barbie furniture, an eiderdown lying on a messy heap on the wooden floor, books and dolls scattered everywhere and in the centre of it all, two little girls fuming at each other.

"I don't see her yet, Yasmine Ebrahim!" one said, planting chubby hands on her hips.

"She will be here, have patience, silly!" said the other one, sticking her tongue out. "And don't yell! Mama or Papa will hear us and come and discover our secret!"

That was my cue, I realized with a smile. So, I blinked and felt a ripple shimmer through my body, all the way from the roots of my hair to my toenails.

The chubby girl looked over her friend's shoulder and gasped when she saw me materialize.

"Ga...ga...ga...ga....GHOSSSST!" *she exclaimed, but the curly haired girl with her back to me quickly planted her hand over her friend's mouth.*

Then, cool as a cucumber, she turned around and smiled at me, showing two missing teeth at the front.

"Hello Ainee!" *she greeted me.* "You are here at last! We thought you would never come!"

CHAPTER NINE

Saturday
1425pm

"Ainee?" I asked, my hallucination crumbling to replace Samiya seated in front of me, still in the same stance I had left her in minutes before.

"Yes," she looked up, slowly lifting her hand from my sweaty palm. "That's what you said when you saw her enter through your open window."

I shook my head, troubled. Climbing off the bed, I took a few steps to glance at my reflection in the mirror.

It was as if I was peering at an old friend and not myself; the hair, the broad forehead, the almond-shaped eyes, the small, straight nose underneath and the heart shaped mouth.

Delicate, feminine features of a child on the verge of entering womanhood in a few years.

But, I thought, leaning closer to stare into the sapphire-flecked brown eyes. This body was stuck in time. The vision...no the memory I had just opened had shown me a girl almost identical to the one in the reflection...and that memory was nearly three years old.

"Samiya, this body has not grown since that day, has it?" I whispered, looking past my reflection into Samiya's one which was observing me from the bed.

"Well, you have grown a little bit," she remarked, bringing her index finger and thumb close.

"It's hardly enough, Samiya," I said, opening my mouth and running my tongue over the gap where two teeth had fallen three years ago.

Two stubs had grown in their place, and it seemed like they would never grow into full-sized teeth. Something was halting the growth of my body.

I turned to look at my friend thoughtfully.

"Tell me more about Ainee…" I urged her. "I feel she is an important link to everything!"

Samiya frowned. "I wish I could forget her. She was like a bad sign or something? I got the creeps when I saw her, but you were gibbering to her like she was your best friend!"

"Samiya, what was she? Was she human?"

Samiya shuddered and hugged herself. "You told me she was your friendly fairy-friend. But I think she was more than that."

Black dogs barking ferociously and rushing like the wind on a cobbled drawbridge….a snake slithering quietly towards a particular house…a beautiful blue female rising from the ground…blue as the heart of a smokeless fire….

"She was weird." Samiya said. "She wanted you to go somewhere with her. She kept talking to you, making signs, but only you could understand her…to me it was like she was speaking under water or something."

BAM!

"Come with me, it is time for me to show you the treasures that I promised!" I said, smiling falsely, trying to captivate the girl with my mystical charm.

She was all innocence and cream. She smiled her hypnotizing little gap-toothed smile and nudged her sceptic friend.

"Come on, Samiya! Say hello, smile! Ainee is my friend. She won't hurt you."

"B…b…but what is she?"

The chestnut-haired angel looked at me and rolled her eyes as if she and I shared a common joke.

Little did she know she shared more than that with me, I thought to myself sadly.

Time was running out. I whispered to my little friend that I needed to get her to the treasure place now, or she would never ever see it again.

"It's a once in a lifetime opportunity!" I lied through my teeth.

"But what about my friend Samiya, we can't just leave her here!"

I clicked my teeth in impatience. The stout little friend could tag along if she wished. I didn't care about her. And I'm sure my liege wouldn't either.

"Aunt Mariam, me and Yas are going over to mine to complete our project!" Samiya sang out as she and Yasmine edged out the backdoor and into the approaching twilight.

"Wait!" Mariam called out. "It's nearly time for **Maghrib**-*the fourth prayer of the day!*"

"That's ok Mama!" Yasmine yelled. "We'll be there just before! Don't you worry about us! I'll see you just after Isha- the final prayer of the day!"

"Grab your jackets! It's getting chilly out there!" Mariam gave in finally.

I watched the whole exchange take place from outside the living room window.

I saw Mariam shake her head and resume her laundry folding in front of the evening news.

So far, so good, I thought.

I glided towards where the two girls were, down the path, panting in exultation at the thought of slipping out on a forbidden adventure.

"Where is she? Where'd she go?" The friend's unease in me was beginning to give me a headache.

I floated right in front of Samiya and blinked into visibility, nearly making her jump out of her skin.

"Are you ready?" I asked her.

She stared at me stupidly.

"Sure, Ainee!" Yasmine spoke up and gave me a hug around my waist.

An unborn sob choked my throat, but I persevered with my plan.

I winked and concentrated. My body flickered slightly and then began to mutate.

Samiya clapped a hand to her mouth, her eyes growing wider and wider as my body changed.

Yasmine looked triumphant. "See what did I tell you, Sam? She is a fairy with super powers!"

My head jutted out, my hair weaved itself into a thick black braid, and my hands fell flat on the ground and sprouted hooves.

"Oh. My. Gawd!" Samiya gawked.

"She's a horse, beautiful like Black Beauty!!!" Yasmine, bless her sweet courage and naïve admiration, clapped her hands in glee, her eyes glowing with excitement.

I whinnied shrilly and motioned for the girls to climb onto my back.

Bending, I watched as Yasmine helped an unwilling and quivering Samiya mount my back, before confidently and gently climbing up herself.

"Hang on tight!" I said before setting out on a gallop into a beautiful, dying sunset.

❄ ❄ ❄

"And then I fainted." Samiya said flatly.

"Wha…" I was giddy with the momentum of the scene I had just witnessed.

Blinking away tears of exhaustion, I focused on Samiya's deadpan features.

"I fainted," she repeated. "And when I awoke next, I was lying in Tillman's Gorge. You were beside me, all knocked out. And your Dad was there sprawled next to us.

"I don't know how he ended up there, but I thought he had been knocked out too? Well, before anything else happened, our folks came in their cars and all hell broke loose. Your Dad…your Dad was confirmed dead by the

Imam and your Mama was afraid you had gone too. I remember your face. You were so white and barely breathing – I thought you were dead also. And your friend…your fairy friend had disappeared." Her voice had sunk into despair.

I took in a huge breath and felt like I was going to be sick.

"I'm sorry Yasmine, but that's the whole story. I don't know what happened in between and people have asked me, hounded me for a year, the police, the Imam, my parents, but I can't remember. That is why I said your Dad would be the best person to clue you in- only he's dead."

I didn't reply. My throat felt so dry, and it was as if I had swallowed needles.

"Please don't ever bring this up again, Yas, ever! It's killing me. I was so freaked out when you started acting weird too, I thought I would go mad and when you asked me today to recount the whole episode of that night, I was so sure I would die!" she paused, tears seeping out of eyes that had witnessed a lot for her age.

"But I feel much better now, Yas, I really do. I think I needed to talk the whole thing through with someone, and who could have understood it better than you? I'm so sorry I ignored you, Yasmine. I should have stuck with you stronger than ever before! It would have done us both good!"

She hugged me, still crying softly.

I was as rigid as a statue though. My heart thudded, my lungs breathed, my eyes blinked – and I felt like I was trespassing on valuable property.

After an embrace that lasted a minute, Samiya sniffed, swiped at her nose and climbed off the duvet.

"Let's wash our faces and go down," she said attempting to smile.

"Everyone must be wondering why we are still up here."

I motioned for her to use the washroom first.

When she'd left the room, I giddily walked on stolen feet towards the mirror again.

The reflection of a few minutes ago – three years ago- stared back at me.

"Ainee," I said softly, staring into the bright unyielding eyes. "Where's Yasmine? What have you done with her?"

CHAPTER TEN

Saturday
2000 hrs

The great boulder in my mind had shifted even more, but the trail of light seeping in wasn't the comfort I had thought it would be.

Lunch had been a successful affair for Mama and she was serenely happy long after the guests had left. The only glitch was Aboodi.

"I need to have a word with you, young man!" she said when the front door slammed shut just after sunset and my brother tried to skulk upstairs.

He looked at us seated by the fire in the living room and reluctantly shrugged his coat off and dumped it on the bottom step of the staircase.

"I'm tired, Ma, can this wait till tomorrow?" he feigned an exaggerated yawn and placed one foot on the second stair.

Mama stood up and the rocking chair she was seated in, reeled back with such force, it banged against the bookshelf.

"Abdallah," she said in a quiet voice that emanated venom. "I said, come here."

The indifferent expression on my brother's face evaporated.

"I want to know what you do for hours at the club whenever you can snatch a free moment." Mama narrowed her eyes.

I watched the exchange going on with something akin to boredom. As tangible as the tension was in the air at that moment, I felt that the tension I was submerged in deserved worldwide recognition.

"Mama, can I be excused," I said, putting my unread book down. "I need to go to bed."

She neither acknowledged my request nor did it seem like my presence was needed here anyway. This was not my fight.

I walked past her and headed towards the stairs, feeling Aboodi's pleading eyes linger on my bowed head, begging me to not leave him alone with a feral animal.

I didn't look up, nor did I decrease my gait. Let him be the matador for a change.

I brushed past him apathetically, feeling no love for this 'brother' of mine who very seldom showed any affection to anything beyond a centimetre radius of his body.

I threw myself into bed, fully clothed, and turned off my night light.

I was eager to go back to sleep, eager to uncover the sequel to the discoveries I had made earlier that day.

Ainee, I thought, twisting the name in my mind and enunciating it with my tongue.

Ainee. Yasmine. Ainee. Yasmine. I was lost between the two. I was both of them and neither at the same time.

Yasmine, I said, talking to myself. "Yasmine, if you're in there please speak to me, I need you. I need to know what happened and why I am in you. I'm so sorry. Forgive me Yasmine. I don't remember. Please, please speak to me…"

The voice in my head which had been bugging me for months, decided to stay deathly quiet.

I closed my eyes, feeling more disturbed and alone than ever.

Sleep, I commanded myself, sleep and the answers shall come.

❄ ❄ ❄

When I next opened my eyes, it wasn't a dream I had hoped to be in.

It was a bright morning and the sun streamed down on a city that was bathed in the aftermath of a violent battle.

A large fire had ripped through the entire area, definitely not the work of either human army, and flames were still licking the air where scores of my people hovered, watching the destruction below.

"The Greeks were always a jealous race," scoffed my leader Zeenon, his huge arms folded across his massive chest.

His Deputy stroked his stubbled chin in thought. "The Persians have lost Persepolis to them. " He mused. "The Greek King has taken control of it."

Zeenon turned to him and smiled, as the flames lapped at the countless bodies strewn below.

"That's the general idea, Veer. The Greeks think they have won with the capture of Persepolis and the defeat of the Persian King and the valuable literature underneath. They also think they are invincible because they have found a new treasure worth the whole world twice over.

"In truth they are the ultimate losers. They are still smarting over the burning of the Acropolis of Athens and anything they seize into their power is a big victory for them. They just don't know what they now hold is going to bring them ultimate destruction."

Veer frowned. "But the treasure…it is worth the world and everything beyond. Isn't that right?"

Zeenon barely nodded to affirm his Deputy's statement.

"That was our plan all along. Persuade the Persians to believe in us, worship us, and give us their all. In the end we reward them with a wife from amongst us who will give them a child worth more than their feeble minds can fathom.

Then we goad the Greeks into avenging the Persians as foretold by the stars.

At the last moment, when it appears that the Greeks are being defeated, we storm in and fight with them, against the Persians and help the Greeks come into contact with what they believe to be their rightful prize."

"But why should the child be reared up by them – the Greeks?" asked Veer.

"Because this present Macedonian King will bide with us well. It has been foretold he will capture many lands and impart his beliefs, traditions and stories in each of them.

The child will grow to have roots spread all over the world. This is our intention."

"But Vesta is heartbroken her human spouse has been killed in the uproar!" Veer pointed out.

"She is strong. She will pull through. She knew from the beginning that she had to let go of her husband and child for the greater good. Her grief will pass."

Zeenon looked around, his eyes searching for something. "Where is that little brat? She should take Vesta her midmorning meal before it gets too late."

He suddenly spotted me hiding behind a shrub, and an evil leer spread across his face.

Suddenly I felt like a rope was tugging at an invisible ring around my nose and pulling- pulling hard.

I yelped in sheer agony and felt the rope drag me forward, squealing and tumbling clumsily, until I reached my Leader-my Master's feet.

"Ainee, you stupid, pathetic creature! Eavesdropping on military secrets now are you, little scum?

Do you want cattle droppings for your meal again! Or would you rather go without anything at all!"

I was crying. Giant tears slid down my thin, bony cheeks, mercilessly showcasing my fear and weakness.

"Go get the food ready for the Mistress. She has enough sorrow already without having to depend on the unworthy likes of you! Filthy creature!"

He spat on the ground.

I recoiled in shame and fright.

There was a tic in the Deputy's cheek, but he maintained his stony expression, his cold eyes glancing elsewhere.

"Now, what are you staring at?" Zeenon barked at me, and angry flames leapt from his eyes. "Get going!"

I sniffled and shrank back into the shrubs again before willing myself to change shape into an animal that could satisfactorily scourge for food.

"Stupid vermin." I heard Zeenon retort to Veer. "I wish I had an older, more sophisticated slave than this cheap piece of dirt. But the only reason I acquiesced was because she was deemed too stupid to pass on our secrets to anyone. I'm thankful for it."

Both men moved onto the topic of the recent bloodshed and I was soon a forgotten matter.

Sadly, I looked away, remembering for the umpteenth time the wise, kind and noble face of the leader of the rival clan, wishing I was his slave instead.

CHAPTER ELEVEN

Time Immemorial

The Mistress Vesta was a striking and forbidding personality in both realms.

The knowledge of her getting married to a member of the "superior species" elevated her and made her renowned even before news of an heiress in the offing, hit our ears.

She was an important link to the continuation of the worship of our kind by "their kind" and the advent of a child whose blood was generated from both worlds would prove to be a massive asset to us.

"I never thought giving up a child, even for a noble reason, would hurt this much," she was moaning, as I brought her a plate of leftovers of some Palace meals.

The higher the caste, the more noble the food, and the high-ranking ones of our kind would enjoy the meaty remains of human provisions scavenged from their very kitchens sometimes.

Sadly, for those in my position, we would be lucky just to get a whiff of such exotic food, like I was doing so just then.

A couple of Mistress Vesta's handmaidens, wide eyed, delphinium blue females forever at her service, numbly listened to their Lady's weeping.

"They tell me, every second generation a female child is born to my bloodline, they shall bring her up to our kingdom to live with us. My mind sees the importance of keeping my Alaira down there amongst those barbarians, but my heart cannot endure it."

I cleared my throat to indicate the food had arrived.

The noble lady didn't even look up.

"Why oh why?" she wept and fresh tears ran down her pale blue cheeks.

"Silence, noble sister!" boomed a stentorian voice and I paled into invisibility on instinct, just in time to see Lord Veer blink into the Mistress's quarters.

"I can hear you moping all the way to Abyssinia!" he said, eyes wide with unkempt fury. "Are you trying to rebel against Lord Zeenon's plans? Did you just dare to question him?"

"No, no..." her head jerked up and her swollen eyes flashed with fear. "I never ever would..."

"Good!" Veer snapped. "Don't let me hear another word of your "heart cannot endure" drivelling! You agreed to perform this task like a loyal follower of Zeenon's Order. You gave yourself in disguised human form to King Cyrus the fifth in matrimony and knew beforehand the plot that would unravel shortly. You were chosen above all women to perform this task and at one time you were proud of it! What ails you now?"

"My brother!" answered the Mistress, her hands clasped in front of her as if in prayer. "Indeed, I felt all that you have just spoken of and more! I willingly concurred to be a big part of your resourceful scheme...but I never expected that I would have feelings for the human and also be in such excruciating agony to part with my one and only child!"

"Excruciating agony, you have not yet experienced dear, foolish sister, for you have not met the wrath of Zeenon!" Veer gritted his teeth. "If I were to confide in him, then my only sister would be in grave danger for treason! Do you honestly think that pitiful human would have really adored you had he known of your true form? How gullible you are! He was merely a tool to shape the vehicle that now sits down there awaiting orders to spread the message!"

"My daughter..." she sniffed, and a sob choked her throat.

"...Is half us and half of them, and a more powerful form than her on earth I cannot conceive of. She will spread the message of us fire-beings in the face of good versus evil...she will promote bloodshed and infidelity, chaos and greed....she will continue the work of our kind from a vantage point, she will do great good to help *'guide'* those fickle creatures down there. You have every right to be HAPPY for her – for all her descendants and all of us!"

I could not bear to hear any more.

Feeling sick to the bottom of my heart, I blinked out of the place, hoping to land somewhere far, far away...at least until I was summoned by my Master.

Monday morning
0800

My eyes opened as the long and exhilarating chapter in my head came to a momentary closure.

The sun was shining outside my window and I gazed for a few seconds at the pattern of the curtain imprinted on my wall.

"Ahem," said someone to my left.

With a start, I jerked to a sitting position, drawing the bedclothes to my chin.

"Assalamu alaikum, darling," said Yasmine's mother. She was seated in the far corner, observing me with red-rimmed eyes and a worried expression.

I just stared at her, my chin trembling, unable to reply to her greeting.

"How…how long have you been seated there, watching me?" I whispered, my heart thudding loudly in my ears, my mind frightened at the thought of Yasmine's mother knowing my identity.

"About twenty-four hours, "she replied calmly, her eyes never leaving my face.

"Wha-"But today was Sunday. I had just gone to sleep last night. Mariam must be pulling my leg, I frantically hoped. Her expression was creeping me out.

"You've been sick, darling," she whispered, and my anxiety ebbed a little. Sickness was not something I was privy to, not in this body at least.

"Oh," I said, rubbing a hand over my cold, damp neck. I suddenly realized I was bathed in a cold sweat and even my hair was sticky.

"You've been slipping in and out of a delirious fever the whole of Sunday, Yasmine," Mariam said, watching my agitation grow with my damp, strewn surroundings.

"But today is Sunday!" I argued vehemently. "I just went to bed last night and…"

"You were rolling and muttering nonsense in your sleep," Mariam continued as if I had not spoken. "I called the doctor. He could not tame you. Then I called the Imam."

"What!" I exclaimed, my eyes wide in horror. An image of the burly, bear-like man bending over my limp, unconscious form, sent shivers up my spine. "You brought him here? In my bedroom? What about my privacy!?"

"It's good he came," Mariam continued, her voice equally rising in tempo. "He was able to motivate me into doing something I stopped doing when your father passed away. I should have never left it, but I was a fool. A weak, undeserving fool!"

My heart stopped just then.

"When your father passed away, I stopped praying to God. I felt betrayed, beaten. He was everything to me, your father. I gave up. I became lost.

"The Imam said God didn't need our prayers. It was we who needed to pray for ourselves. The soul was created in a form of submission and it's us humans who choose to stay on the path or stray from it. For so long I have strayed, Yasmine. I have opened the doors for *Shaitan* to come and play his dirty games. The Imam said I should have gotten a wake-up call the day you came back to life after your yearlong battle with an unnamed sickness. I didn't. I took it for granted.

"But when you went through a similar scenario yesterday...that was when I got a jolt! That was when I realized it was I who had left God and not the other way around. I was given a reminder once, twice, but never paid heed...Yasmine, I don't want to lose you too....together we are going to change...we are going to be the Muslims we are meant to be!

"Just because I wear the *hijaab*, I don't get a ticket to *Jannah*- Paradise. I have to earn it! Yes, Yasmine! Today we are going to change, all of us! Our God is a merciful God to keep reminding us to turn to Him and He will shower us with His Infinite blessings! May this sickness be a blessing in disguise and bring us back to Him, *Aameen*!"

I watched my mother's face change from a pallid deadpan mask to one of sizzling excitement.

She had left her chair and was now seated on the edge of my bed, looking expectantly into my face.

"Sure Ma-"I stopped. Mariam. Mama was now a foreign word on my tongue. I had not known my mother for hundreds of human years.

"But what did the Imam say when he saw me?" I asked her.

She raised an eyebrow. "The Imam said there was nothing that a good dose of Quranic verses couldn't do to heal you."

I froze again.

"But your fever broke just as he was about to recite the longest chapter of the Holy Quran. And he got an urgent call at the same time from Layla saying there was a small accident in the kitchen at home. So, he had to rush back. However, he did say that he would come again tonight and check on you. In the meantime, I am going to cleanse the house with some Quran tapes!"

Deep beneath the phony smile I was emitting, panic rushed to and fro. But in the meantime, I had another problem to solve.

"Ma- uh...Mom, can you give me a quick ride to school? I promised Samiya I would help her out with something today!"

CHAPTER TWELVE

Monday
0840 am

Despite Mariam's valiant attempts at thwarting me from going to class today, I was out the door and heading to the car, fully dressed, in less than half an hour.

"Mama! I'm telling you, I'm perfectly all right now!" I insisted. "I need to be outta the house and getting some fresh air! And I did promise Samiya I'll be with her today!" There was something about keeping a covenant that was etched deep in my soul.

"But Yasmine! You were near death, only yesterday! You need to rest, you need to recover fully! I'm sure Samiya will understand!" Mariam refused to budge out the front door.

"Fine, Ma!" I lashed out, feeling annoyed. "I'll walk all the way! And woe betide you if I get sick and die on the side of the road in this freezing cold!"

She quickly grabbed the car keys.

I felt bad I had to speak to her the way I did and deliver another emotional blow to her, but that couldn't be helped.

She gave birth to this body and not to the soul that is in it right now. She is not your mother. You don't have to feel sorry for her, I tried to placate myself. Strangely, that didn't make me feel any less troubled.

I stole a glance to the left, while Mariam drove me to school, tight-lipped and bleary-eyed.

My heart-or was it Yasmine's- thudded painfully in my chest as I realized how much this woman loved her daughter.

I could not remember anyone having loved me in this manner.

She had stayed up the whole night to wait for my fever to break...she was willing to become more pious....I was sure the list would go on.

As Mariam maneuvered the Ford through the fresh snow-kissed roads of Sand Point, I tried to open Yasmine's memories like I had done earlier, to uncover more of this mother-daughter bond.

Only now I could not do so at will. Her memories seemed to be shut in a book too heavy for me to open.

With a sinking heart I realized that as my own memories were awakening, and my own soul was getting stronger, Yasmine was slowly fading away.

She had not spoken to me for quite a while. Now I knew the source of that conflicting voice in my head, I wanted it back. I wanted to know for certain that the little girl was safe and sound is spite of the parasite occupying her body.

"Here we are," Mariam declared as she skidded to a stop beside the school gates. "I shall call the school every two hours to see if you're okay, do you get me?" she asked fiercely.

I nodded.

"I understand you want to get out of the house and live normally, and that is the only reason I let you out the front door, but believe me baby, if I could, I would keep you safe in my arms till whatever it is that's gripping you will be gone for good! Do you understand?"

I inhaled sharply. "Yes,"

She clasped my hands and looked deep into my eyes, and I could feel her trying to reach into my soul.

"I love you, darlin'," she whispered, and promptly, a tear shone in each eye.

"I love you too," I replied, and surprisingly it wasn't hard for me to fake emotion. I only wished this wonderful human being would find place in her heart to love me for myself too.

I dashed into the school hall just as the first bell stopped ringing.

First period English, first period English, I panted to myself as I ran towards the classroom.

I reached the door just as my teacher, Mr. Moore also arrived at it.

"Well, well, well, Miss Ebrahim, just in the nick of time, are we?" he said, raising an amused brow above his broad spectacles.

I opened my mouth to deliver a readily available excuse when he winked at me and opened the door for me to walk in.

"No excuses in the hallways, Miss Ebrahim! For I usually make mine up once I'm already inside the classroom..."

He smiled broadly, and I flashed back a weaker replica as I walked into the noisy pre-first-period atmosphere.

My eyes immediately began searching for Samiya.

It wasn't too hard to spot a glimpse of a moping, cringing, scarf-toting girl right at the back of the class, surrounded by a gaggle of jeering girls and inquisitive boys.

I drew in breath to yell, Leave her alone! Respect her for her choice in life! But Mr. Moore beat me to it with his much milder vocalization.

"Settle down class! And Good Morning to you all too!"

Agitatedly I watched as the cluster of kids around Samiya broke away and joined their seats.

I'm sorry I'm late, I mouthed to Samiya, just as her face came into view. But to my utter surprise, she wasn't crying, nor did she look like she had been bullied.

She didn't even see me. Her widely expressive eyes were focused on Alisa Mahn, who from three seats away, was miming at her to exchange telephone numbers.

I was flabbergasted as I continued to see another girl give Samiya the thumbs-up, and yet another one call in a stage whisper to her partner, "I'm gonna ask my mama to get me one of those for the spring festival!"

"Ahem," someone cleared his throat from behind me, and I whirled around, still stuck in a daze.

"Ready whenever you are, Miss Ebrahim," It was Mr. Moore, gesturing to my empty seat, while the whole class, already in their places, laughed at what they thought was my absent-mindedness.

I threw one last, forlorn gaze at Samiya before taking my seat, but once again, she did not acknowledge my presence.

CHAPTER THIRTEEN

Monday
1100 hrs

PE period was graced with the presence of popular personality and interstate ice hockey coach, Burt Reynolds.

A vast number of kids from grades seven till ten, with signed slips of permission, were taken to the Sand Point outdoor skating rink where the famous Coach would demonstrate the basics of the game.

The ice rink, I gathered from a shadow of a dying memory, was a place that had been frequently visited by the Ebrahims when the father had still been alive.

So, these legs knew how to skate, I mused, but will the force that resides in them be able to execute the action? Twitching my toes inside my shoes, I waited with the other kids on the bleachers.

Coach Reynolds was an average sized man with broad shoulders and a faint Canadian accent that clashed with his Idahoan roots.

He cleared his throat from the front of the bleachers and began an introductory speech on the game of ice hockey.

I looked around me and found Samiya not far off, seated at a higher angle, yakking nineteen to a dozen with Alisa Mahn and her entourage. I also didn't miss the fact that Mikaela, Keisha and Madison, her usual groupies, were nowhere to be seen.

"… is a full contact sport and body checks are allowed, injuries can be a quite common." The coach was saying. "Protective gear is highly recommended and is enforced in all competitive situations. This usually includes a helmet, shoulder pads, elbow pads, a mouth guard, protective gloves, hockey pants, athletic cup, shin pads, skates, and also a neck protector, though that is optional…but we won't be throwing ourselves into a full game today. Instead, with the help of my assistant coaches, Kerry Whitehall and Kirk Runaway, and also with the supervision of your PE teacher, we shall be observing how you hold yourself on the ice during warm-ups."

There was a slight buzz of voices as everyone geared up and was sorted by gender into two groups.

"We shall start with Group 1. Please divide yourselves into two teams, boys." the coach said. "This is just so I can practically explain to you the rules while also teaching you the tips and tricks of the trade. This is not a win-lose match, do you understand. Girls, please wait in the bleachers till I call you forward. Ok now, are we ready?"

There was a chorus of "Yah!"s and I watched dreamily, knowing that it would be a while before teams C and D would be cast in the rink.

There was a burst of laughter from behind me and I flipped around to see Samiya throwing her head back in mirth as Alisa whispered something to her.

"Girls! Girls!" Ms Bellinski blew her whistle, one sharp piercing sound directed at Samiya and the crowd. "Just because you are seated waiting, doesn't mean you don't pay attention to what's going on down there!"

"Sowwy, Ms. Bellinski.." Alisa pouted, while her admiring followers snorted or tried to pinch their lips to keep from laughing out loud.

Ms. Bellinski could not have heard the jibe, for she just shook her head and turned around to focus on the bustling activity within the rink.

There was a slight wind blowing downwards and I could catch snippets of the conversation taking place above me.

"...this weekend so will you be able to come?" Alisa's honeyed voice was saying.

"Will there be boys at the party?" there was a waver in Samiya's deeper tone, and I could see her mind already calculating an excuse to give her mother.

"Of course, girlfriend!" Alisa's sickeningly sweet voice again, hiccupping with disbelief. "We are twelve after all! Nearly teenagers! I persuaded my mom to let me invite boys to my party and she was like, 'sure hon, aren't you growing up fast!' She was mighty easy!"

"My Mom gave in after a few scuffles," said another girl. "What matters is that in the end we have fun! Who cares if we step on a few toes to get it?"

A few girls tittered.

I listened with bated breath as Samiya made a decision.

"Sure, um, I...I think my Mom will be all for it too!" she said, covering up her stuttering with a layer of faux enthusiasm.

"Excellent!" Alisa's voice sent prickles up my arms. "And don't forget to wear your er...hee-jayb thingy."

"*Hijaab*." Samiya corrected her.

"Yeah. Whatever." I could picture Alisa shrugging nonchalantly, tossing her gleaming blond ponytail over her shoulders. "So, we'll expect to see you then! Catch ya later!"

The girls disbanded, and I straightened up in my seat as my acute hearing picked up a pair of boots heading down my way.

Samiya would have walked right past me if I hadn't called out to her.

"Oh." She said, turning around and looking confused to see me there. "Er...hi Yasmine! Didn't see you there!"

"Hey, Samiya," I smiled for both of us. "Settling well in the new attire?"

Her eyes glazed uncomprehendingly. "Uh?"

I looked pointedly at her hijab. A faint blush stole over her cold cheeks. "Oh, aah, this...yeah...cool."

"I'm sorry I was late today," I said, my eyes not leaving her face. "I was running a fever of one hundred and three degrees the whole of yesterday and had to force Mama to let me come today. I panicked the whole way to school, thinking you were being molested. I was ready to keep my end of the promise, Samiya. But I see that you have not only forgotten me – again- but also your old friends." I gestured to Keisha seated by herself in the bleachers, solemnly studying from a book, and Mikaela and Madison who were doing individual warm up exercises further down.

Samiya followed my gloved hand, and then looked sheepishly at her feet. From the rink, whistles blew, and people were rushing at each other with hockey sticks.

"Look," she said at last. "I thought I would be the laughing stock today, but I was wrong. The most popular girl in school wants to be my best buddy now! I have envied her for years! And so have you Yasmine, in case you've forgotten." That was a taunt, but I brushed it aside.

"But Alisa is up to something," I said earnestly. "You can't seriously be thinking about going to her party Saturday night!"

"You eavesdropped on us?!" she remarked, her eyes blazing in disbelief.

"That's beside the point," I said. "Also, if you were speaking loud enough for others to hear it, it's not my fault."

"Whatever!" she said, tossing her head in perfect imitation of the Snob Queen. "Listen, Yasmine, don't try to threaten me, OK? We had our little talk the other day, now that's all over. I told you all I knew and in the end you didn't even have to stick up for me today, so in truth, you still owe me one, and not the other way around. So stop looking at me like I have made a mistake! If I'm going to the party, that's my business. So please just back off!"

She turned and stomped downwards, where I mutely watched her take a seat in the front row, close to Ms. Bellinski and some other kids from the second round.

I shook my head and noticed Keisha observing me from the left. She put down her book and tilted her lips in the smallest of smiles, one that jabbed at the wall of ice that had been erected between us for over a year.

I smiled back at her, feeling that somewhere in either my life or Yasmine's I had heard a saying, "Smile often, because smiling is a form of charity."

CHAPTER FOURTEEN

Monday
1300 hrs

PHOOOOOOOOEEEEEEEEEEEE! The whistle was blown, and we were off.

After an hour of analysing our carriage and movement on the ice, Coach Reynolds decided we were ready to use the hockey sticks and play a casual game.

"Remember, hockey is an offside game," Coach Reynolds said. "This means, forward passes are allowed unlike certain other games like rugby or even hockey played in the past. Remember, no bodily contact with the puck or with yourselves. It is not permissible unless in involuntary situations. It is also known as body checking, which marks a minor or sometimes major penalty.

"I shall now throw the puck on the ice. Please position yourselves into two straight rows facing each other. You shall first attempt to pass the puck back and forth and practice hand-eye coordination before we continue further."

He reached into his bag and pulled out a small disk of vulcanized rubber.

I looked at the opponent in front of me and realized that inadvertently I had been cast with Alisa Mahn.

Her poisonous green eyes gleamed menacingly under her helmet.

"Okay girls, this is not a game, just a practice at passing, so lemme see how your posture is...that's right, bend forward a bit...okay, we'll begin from the left."

The puck skid along the ice and was lapped up by a burly ninth grade girl, who shot it far too fast for her opponent to catch it with her stick.

A chorus of catcalls echoed from the group of boys watching us from the bleachers.

"Not too fast," Coach Reynolds advised, as he fluidly skated across to demonstrate the right move.

"Hello, loser," hissed Alisa and I turned to face her gloating expression.

"Prepared to cower behind a ninth grader like a mouse when it's our turn?" she asked.

"I think I can hold my own," I said quietly.

"Sure," she snorted, a vile smile lifting up the corner of her full lips. "You are the only fourth grader here, midget. I'm surprised they didn't kick you out as soon as they saw you. You'll be halibut bait before you know it. Quit now while you still have your uh...dignity."

"What evil tricks have you up your sleeve for Saturday night's party, Alisa?" I switched topics.

She wasn't taken aback at all. Her lovely face stretched into a sinister smile and she raised a beautifully arched brow in mockery.

"None of your business, dwarf-girl. Why don't you worry about your little Barbie dolls' tea party instead? I'm sure there are tons for you to do without thinking outside your league."

"Samiya is way within my league, Alisa," I said softly, my eyes boring into her in rage. "If you harm her…"

Alisa threw back her head and trilled in laughter. "If I harm her, brat, there's nothing you or your puny little plastic toys can do about it, so chill!"

Just then the puck slid to me.

I raised my eyes to meet Alisa's and both of us crouched forward, all set for a battle we both knew was about to begin.

The whistle blew.

I swung my stick and it sent the puck whizzing towards Alisa.

She caught it and sent it flying over my head and toward the empty goal behind me.

"Too far!" Coach Reynolds said, raising his hands in the air.

But I looked at Alisa and smiled without affection. She raised an eyebrow, challenging me.

Ignoring the booing crowd outside the rink and the calls of the coaches within, I raced off towards the net, my skates cutting furious arcs in the ice. Any doubts I had about synchronizing my blank mind to Yasmine's body memory of skating fluttered away as I expertly flew on the wings of vengeance.

I stopped the puck just in time and wheeled around with perfect grace.

Alisa skated towards me with power bent to match mine, her hockey stick and confidence forever poised.

"You won't win, Alisa," I muttered, gritting my teeth.

"Try and stop me," she said, her turn to deliver an icy smile.

I sent the puck flying to the other side of the rink in a move that was too fast for her eyes to follow. Both of us raced towards it, ignoring the shrill whistles and commands of an angry Coach Reynolds.

"Who do you think you are, midget?" she screeched as we raced on our skates, caught in our own whirlwind of competition.

The ice-rink vanished before my eyes and I was racing in the air as far away as I could get from my clan.

I raced past glittering minarets of Arabian fortresses, laughing maniacally, blinked in and out of snowy regions in uncontrollable tears, and skimmed over the tops of low-lying dwellings, all the time in a frenzy to escape from myself and the helpless circumstances I was trapped in.

Finally, I settled on some dew-drenched blades of grass, in the form of my favourite earth creature- a black python, and slithered aimlessly into a mossy alcove.

I was beyond laughter or tears and was confused to the point of splitting into two.

I caught the puck and panted, staring daggers into Alisa's eyes.

"I will not let you score a goal, ever, Alisa Mahn." I shouted, my anger infused with a much deeper meaning.

"Shut up, weenie slime bag!" Alisa roared, her cheeks red and her nostrils flared.

Help me, I need help, I want out! I cried to myself as I slunk in erratic patterns over the grass.

"Assalamu Alaikum- peace be upon you- fair one," a voice said from somewhere.

I inhaled sharply and looked around, wondering who had invaded my privacy.

To my right, another snake was slithering forward. He was larger and glimmered with authority right down to the last little scale.

With a sharp beat of my heart I recognized him to be the leader of the rival clan – the one I fantasized about ever since the manipulated war.

"What are you crying about?" he asked, stopping at a modest distance from me.

"Nothing," I replied.

❄ ❄ ❄

"This is preposterous!" Coach Reynolds barked, as Alisa and I still snarled at each other, lost in the throes of our own heated little brawl.

"Stop! Stop and return to your places at once!" Assistant coach Runaway clapped his hands and stormed menacingly towards us, scraping angry arcs across the ice.

"Defying orders always gives me a little thrill," Alisa said to me as we raced shoulder to shoulder, the puck skidding just inches in front of us. "But you, midget? You might fall to pieces just thinking about it."

"Do I look like I am in pieces now?" I said to her. My stick struck the puck and I caught it and whirled around to race towards my goal.

"You *sick* little worm," Alisa shouted in anger. "You won't get any bigger. Something's wrong with you! You've got a disease!"

"I'm just a useless slave," I confirmed, after minutes of silence between us. "I can't help being who I am. But I don't like what's going on with my people. They are trying to manipulate the humans below without their knowledge."

He didn't reply. I marvelled at the feeling of power he generated even when he didn't say a word.

"Do you know the story of Sulaiman, a Prophet of God?"

I shook my head.

"Would you like to listen to it?"

"I'm not sure if I should be here," I said, looking around me nervously. *"If my Master knew I was fraternizing with the enemy, I would be killed!"*

"By all means, don't disobey your Master," he said, and another ray of admiration at his fairness burst in my chest. *"But in*

my opinion, I wouldn't call listening to a very special book revealed by God to both mankind and the Jinn, fraternizing.

"Go now if you have to, but if you think you would like to hear a story of truth any time at all, just come here, and in the presence of my sisters I would like to teach you something from this very special book."

I nodded, dazed by the sound of his calm and clear voice. Nobody had ever spoken to me as an equal before. I had not known kindness or compassion. And his words about a book of truth, intrigued me.

"That's the truth, that's why you're a dwarf." Alisa shouted, our growing row a secret no more. "You've got a disease worse than cooties!" I paid no heed to her mounting insults, only intent on scoring a goal.

A balmy afternoon, a different location, ten of us seated in a circle in a forest clearing, visible only to animals who weren't around at the moment.

Our speaker Al Barak was telling us the captivating story of Prophet Sulaiman and his control over Jinns.

"And no time before or after that was a human given such a privilege to bring not only the Jinns, but also ants, birds and even the wind under his command…then there came the time where a barrier was put between our world and theirs, and we pledged that we would not make contact with them anymore…only the more rebellious among us broke this law…"

He recited from the noble book in his hands. "' Proclaim— I have received the divine revelation that some jinns attentively listened to my recitation, so they said, 'We have heard a unique Qur'an. That guides to the path of goodness, we have therefore accepted faith in it; and we shall never ascribe anyone as a partner to our Lord....."

His recitation was of celestial beauty that pierced through my heart and nudged my soul. I shook from head to toe, but did not feel excruciating pain as I had felt during a similar recitation above Persepolis.

"'And that when we heard the guidance, we accepted faith in it; so whoever accepts faith in his Lord, has no fear - neither of any loss nor of any injustice." He looked up and closed the book.

CHAPTER FIFTEEN

Another day…another time, another story was being told.

And yet another.

Day after day I would steal to his territory where I was always welcomed like an equal by his beautiful, humble sisters, and offered simple, beautiful food. Their kind did not intervene in the affairs of human beings but were still able to live in ease and comfort.

"Why am I not treated like the slave I'm supposed to be when I'm with all of you?" I asked, with wonder in my eyes.

He did not look directly at me. Lately he would always look down in what I assumed was a bashful manner - though how could it be for one so great, I wondered – and speak to me in a soft, respectful tone.

"Because in my eyes, you are not a slave," he answered. "We don't believe in slavery anymore."

❄ ❄ ❄

"I don't believe this!" Coach Reynolds looked like he was going to bust a nerve in his neck, and the boys were cheering us on from the stands.

I hesitated for a second and Alisa grabbed the opportunity to steal the puck with her stick and dash towards her end. I followed her in hot pursuit.

I was touched by Al Barak's statement. He smiled at his feet and walked away.

I turned around and reluctantly thought of returning home to my degraded status. I didn't see the reedy creature watching me from behind a prickly bramble.

❄ ❄ ❄

Alisa was gaining speed and even though I pushed with every bleeding drop of my strength, the memories I was simultaneously witnessing, pulled me back.

I didn't want her to score that goal!

I huffed and I puffed, and my leg muscles protested in agony. I didn't want her to score, and this feeling had nothing to with Alisa per se, or the present. And yet I persisted.

"Go Alisa, Go Alisa," boys cheered and whistled from the outside, whereas girls rooted for her on the inside.

And from somewhere in the midst of all the cheering and the screaming, I heard faint voices shout "Go Yasmine, Go Yasmine,"

I didn't know which voices represented the minority in my favour, but that kindled a little flame of hope in my chest.

"Yasmine, Yasmine!" it continued and so did I.

"Ainee! AINEE!" he roared, consumed with paramount madness. He kept heaving at the invisible cord that bound me to him, and it was as if my nose would be torn from my face.

"How dare you, you miserable scum! How dare you tag along with the nemesis and listen to THAT BOOK? How could you? And here I was thinking you were a stupid little ruffian with brains the size of a mustard seed! And all this time…all this time…"

He kicked, swore and spat on me, and during that time he wouldn't let me change into an immaterial form to protect myself from bodily harm.

So, I whimpered and bled, and cried and screamed for mercy, my dog's body nearly spent.

It went on for hours. Zeenon could be as merciless as he wanted to be for as long as he desired and there was nobody to stop him.

As my cries echoed through the seven kingdoms and back, I thought of Al Barak's kindly face and dwelt on the beautiful stories he had taught me.

I focused on the pain of Prophet Ayoob when he was inflicted with difficult trials, both physical and mental.

I recalled the struggles of Prophet Yunus while he was trapped in the whale's belly and his complete submission and faith in God.

I felt a slice of the pain that nameless man had felt when his village people had stoned him to death for trying to teach them good values.

And I thought of Al Barak again and his magnetic voice and smile.

Just before my mind drifted into oblivion, I heard a female voice call out.

"No, my Lordship! Spare her, I beg you! I have a task that would serve as the ideal retribution for her misdeed whilst doing us great good.

"Please sell her to me and let her be my slave. I will ensure that she's the one to bring me my half-human progeny from Earth so that they, as pre-pubescent girls will learn to live with us in our realm."

"And how will that be a punishment for the little mutt, Vesta?" Zeenon 's voice was raspy.

"Well, I had been watching her at those little meetings. I've seen the rapture on her face whenever scriptures of the Book were revealed. I know she thinks she is almost one of their kind now. And their rule number one is: never intermingle with humans. So, when I give her this task, she will have to abide by my rules. She will be forced to go against her wishes. Ultimately she's the loser. She will live for centuries hating herself. And that, I think is a punishment more appropriate than any physical blow you could inflict on her or death itself."

As Zeenon and Vesta laughed, I wished I would die now, so I wouldn't have to wake up to a world without Al Barak and a hell worse than the one I had already been through.

Alisa slammed her stick against the puck and I helplessly watched it sail through the air and come spiralling down again, before skidding into the net.

"SCORE!" she screamed out loud and the crowd screamed with her.

I fell down to my knees; all the wind had been knocked out of me.

"Get up! Get up!" A rough hand seized my arm and yanked me to my quivering feet, not allowing me to rest my defeated limbs.

"Both of you are disqualified from the competition AND I'll make sure the Principal suspends you from school for a week!" barked our gym teacher.

She dragged me towards Alisa and seized her by the sleeve as well.

"Out of the rink, both of you," she growled in fury. "You have shamed the Coach and dishonoured the school! I won't be surprised if you're expelled!"

"So much for your high and mighty words," Alisa whispered to me, once we'd taken off our skates and limped to a standing ovation from the bleachers. "You'll always be a loser."

And it was not Alisa's voice I heard, but the cruel tones of Mother Vesta.

My heart sank, even as I saw out of the corner of my eye, the three people who had cheered me on – Mikaela, Keisha and Madison – look at me sympathetically from the rink.

CHAPTER SIXTEEN

Monday
1300 hrs

"I can't believe this, just yesterday you were practically immobile, and today you are suspended for a week because you couldn't keep still!"

Mariam shook her head incredulously at me, as she gunned the engine.

I sat hunkered in my seat, the collars of my jacket twisted up to hide my face as much as possible from Mariam, from the rest of the world.

"I'm not sure if I should be upset with you, Yasmine." Mariam said, as I stared out the window silently. "I would have never expected you, my cuddly, precious little kitten to have become such a daring little rebel. I'm afraid to voice it – but I think I'm proud of you!"

I looked over at Mariam and she smiled uncertainly at me.

The word 'rebel' sparked an image of Aboodi in my mind. I hadn't seen him after Saturday night's episode.

"Mama, where's Aboodi? Did you guys have a row?"

Her face tautened. "Let's not talk about him now, Yasmine. He's a rebel of a different kind. There's nothing cute or cuddly about his actions.

"He snubbed me off and went to bed when all I wanted to do was ask him why he had set up residence in that stupid youth club, and this earned him a month of grounding."

"Oh," I said simply.

"Yes, and the only time he's allowed out of his room is to come downstairs for his meals and go to school. No other extracurricular activities are permitted."

She swerved the car onto our driveway. "And oh, I think you should be grounded too, young lady, for one week, though, just to prove that my parenting skills are not all bad and I do agree with your teachers one little bit about your raucous behaviour today!"

She patted me on my hooded head and twisted the key out of the ignition.

"Ok, I'm going to fix us a quick sandwich each, and then I've got to get back to work," Mariam said.

"And remember, the TV's out of bounds, so try to keep yourself entertained until your brother or I return in a few hours. And don't turn on the stove if you're hungry after this. Just reach out for something in the pantry…"

"Ok, ok, Mama," I said, flinging my schoolbag on a chair and pushing back my hood. "I think I can manage all right."

"And if there's anything, call me! The work phone number is on the fridge, you know that right?" Mariam said, her hands already busy untying the bread bag and opening jars.

She left in fifteen minutes, parting with the usual dos and don'ts.

The moment I had the house to myself, I ran upstairs to my room.

"Ok, Yasmine, speak to me girl, c'mon!" I coaxed my inner self, as I fell into a cross-legged position in front of my full-length mirror.

A fearful thought entered my mind. What if the latest, vivid memory had snuffed the last of Yasmine's light? What if she was gone forever?

I closed my eyes, took a deep breath and concentrated with all my might to extricate myself from her.

Every hair on my flesh, every fibre of my being responded to the urgent request I sent out, but I was only exerting force on Yasmine's body, whereas my immaterial one was firmly locked inside and holding onto something.

I exhaled and tried again.

And again.

And again.

I let out a cry of frustration when nothing happened. I was still stuck staring at Yasmine's flushed face in the mirror.

"Yasmine…" I said in distress, begging for a word from her, a sigh, a movement – anything.

But she remained as quiet as death.

1800 hrs

Mariam remained true to her word. She restarted her daily prayers, filled the house with tapes of *Qirat*- chapters recited from the Quran- in place of Bon Jovi, and gathered the Quran from its dusty nook in a wall to open it in all its fine glory on the round dining table.

I inched towards it, and looked over her shoulder, eager to feast my eyes on the unique script I had seen hundreds of years ago.

The curling, majestic letters looked blank as they did not flow through a beautiful voice that sent pangs of sorrow ripping at me, for Mariam was stuttering and pausing every now and then in a voice as flat as her Saturday pancakes.

In a way I was grateful I was not driven into a near-trance of rapture like I used to be driven into, when 'he' used to recite to me and the others in front of a crackling fire.

Too many similarities and memories of that brief happy moment in my life would have made me cry on the spot then and there.

"Come, Yasmine," Mama whispered, swivelling around to look at me. "Come, read with me."

But I was illiterate. Only my brain had appreciated through the help of my ears what my eyes had never understood.

Whatever I had to say then was interrupted by the doorbell.

"The Imam and his wife!" Mariam announced, as she opened the door.

The cosiness, warmth and peace in the house were suddenly extinguished, like they had been doused with a bucket of cold, rancid water.

I straightened up and prepared to make an exit when the Imam boomed in his thick, sonorous voice: "Oh, reading the Quran, Maasha Allah!"

"Well, I was just off to bed," I said, trying not to look at him looking at me with those piercing eyes of his.

"Oh, do stay and read for me, please, or if you're very tired sit down and listen to me read." I didn't like the direction this was heading into. He had an ulterior motive, one that led me to believe he was closer to uncovering the very truth that I was frantically trying to hide from everyone else.

"I really am very tired," I insisted, throwing a glance at Mariam, begging her to back me up.

Mariam, even though she was not too happy with my lack of civility, took the hint and thankfully turned towards the Imam.

"She had ice-hockey try-outs today, Imam Yusuf. You have no idea what happened there! I'm sure after I've recounted the story to you over a cup of coffee, you'll agree she needs to have an early night."

I thanked her abundantly with my eyes and turned around to speed upstairs, past Aboodi's firmly shut door, and into my room, all the time feeling the hot blast of the Imam's glare on my back

CHAPTER SEVENTEEN

Tuesday
0100 hrs

My dreams that night were torn, dreadful images of my own immoral past and the path I had chosen to take in my weakness.

I had betrayed Al Barak.

I had sat there drinking in his every word, feeling my mind open up to absorb the wonder he was pouring in, but when the time had come I had turned my back on him, his noble people, the Book and The Supreme Being Himself.

I had chosen to creep back into the darkness of the woods even after I had grasped the hand of the person willing to pull me out of it.

I was the biggest hypocrite ever.

Century after century, I would go down to earth, at her bidding, and bring back a stolen treasure, a pre-pubescent female child, to our realm, to her waiting arms.

More often than not, the frightened girls would pine for their human kin and wither away after a few years of mourning.

But sometimes, the more feisty ones would tap into their dormant fire-genes and attune to their new environment.

But even then, they were still mostly human, and this prevented them from living as long as we did, and time after time, I watched Mother Vesta bend over a deceased 'daughter' and weep endlessly, her heart hardening with every death while alternately fuelling her greed for the right to have a daughter of her own once again.

I woke up, my body convulsed in racking sobs, as the fading images showed Vesta and me hovering over Sand Point Alaska, not too long ago from the present.

"This is our next target, Slave," she said, her voice terribly aged and her eyes sunken in, as if she too were tiring of this monotonous, aimless mission.

"Yes, Mother Vesta," I replied, bowing - weak, submissive, obedient and cowardly as always.

And miserable beyond despair.

Mother Vesta was right. There could not have been a punishment worse than eons of torture to the soul.

Wednesday
0900 hrs

After Mariam and a disgruntled Aboodi had departed for work and school, I threw myself once again into the task of trying to contact Yasmine.

No such luck.

1200 hrs

I made myself a cheese and jelly sandwich while talking on the phone with Mariam, who was nervous I would cut myself with the butter knife.

1400hrs

I scourged through the house looking for family albums but decided Mariam must have thrown them away. Sighing in frustration I tore at my hair. "Serves you right if you find yourself bald by the time you get back!" I screamed at Yasmine, at no one. "Oh, Yasmine, you will get back, won't you? I beg you, please, please return…"

1830pm

At suppertime, over a plate of mashed potatoes and green peas: "Mama, don't we have any photos of Dad?" I asked serenely, not meeting her gaze.

She paused in mid-serve of gravy to her plate. "Why do you ask, Yasmine?"

I could feel Aboodi looking at me for the first time in days, and I felt I would have turned to putty had I met his gaze.

"Because he's my Dad?" I said, shrugging. Isn't it normal for one to ask anyway?

"Yasmine, I told you years ago that the particular subject of your Dad is just as dead as he is." Mariam said coldly.

"But Ma…"

"Stuff it, kid," Aboodi spoke up unexpectedly and his voice sounded hoarse and tense. "It doesn't concern you."

"Mama! Please! He was my Dad. I have the right to know what happened…"

"YASMINE!" the same rage I had seen a week ago resurfaced, only this time, Mariam was staring daggers at ME.

I stiffened in my seat and felt Aboodi react similarly.

"Please continue eating if you don't want to be sent up to your room in disgrace," Mariam said.

I glared back, breathing heavily.

Nothing eventful happened for the rest of the evening. Even my sleep was a dreamless one.

Thursday
0800 hrs

An idea was beginning to form in my head. But, looking at Mariam's thin mouth and unforgiving eyes, I decided I could wait another day perhaps, before implementing it.

Friday
0815 am

"Mama," I said tentatively, over a bowl of oatmeal porridge and a glass of orange juice.

"Mmm…" she was reading the morning newspaper with her customary cup of coffee.

"Mama, I know I'm grounded but can you please give me permission to go to the library." I said. "I am lagging behind in my school work and don't want to be the last in the class this term because of one week of suspension."

Aboodi quizzically looked up at me from his porridge, his thick brows raised ever so slightly.

I focused on Mama's newspaper and then back at her impassive face, hoping she wouldn't reply in the negative.

Aboodi followed my gaze and a light bulb clicked in his head.

No! He mouthed at me.

I ignored him. "Mama?"

She finally put her paper down and looked at me. "What does the library have that we don't?"

"Science books, Mama," I said. "Heaps of them. And tutorials and case studies and I think I have a project in Aleutian History too. Please, Mama. I'd rather do something with my time than just stare at the empty walls."

"You should have thought of that before you got yourself suspended." She remarked coldly, downing the last of her coffee and glaring at me.

Ouch! No more cuddly rebel for her, I thought.

Aboodi was also waiting for her response.

"OK." She said, after half a minute of excruciating anticipation. "But I'm going to drop you there myself and leave word with the librarian that you should remain on their premises until evening, when I return from work to pick you up."

Anything better than staring at my reflection the whole day and willing it to talk to me, I thought.

"Thanks, Mama," I said leaping up to envelop her in a hug.

She didn't hug me back, but I saw her expression soften a bit.

"Why don't you let sleeping dogs lie," Aboodi whispered gruffly to me, once Mariam was out of earshot.

He didn't realize how close to home his words hit.

CHAPTER EIGHTEEN

0900 hrs

"Hi, can I have access to microform footage of any local newspaper covering the months of April, May and June of 1989 please? I would also prefer weekend editions."

The librarian was a heavy-set woman in her late fifties and she looked a cross between a Native and a country bumpkin. She looked down her horn-rimmed glasses at me; a little girl whose head was only slightly above the level of the high counter.

"And why may I ask, do you require the footage?" she asked through her nose, in a pompous voice.

"It's for a school project I'm doing on modern Aleutian history," I replied promptly.

"Why would they make a little fourth grader go to such lengths I wonder," she muttered more to herself, but she did push her chair back with a satisfying creak.

"And what great event happened during that time period that made it crucial for your school to tax their students in such a manner?" she asked, waddling on her heavy ankles towards the back room. "Pray, enlighten me coz I only came here eight months ago. I'm fairly new to this region, even though my ancestors lived here."

"A lot of things," I said, shrugging. "During World War II, Aleuts were evicted from their homeland to the south-east regions of Alaska and most of them died due to various epidemics. It was only in 1989 to 1990 that the Commission on Wartime Relocation and Internment of Civilians paid recompense to the few survivors. "

The librarian was staring open mouthed at me as I finished quoting word to word from my History textbook.

"And I am in the seventh grade," I added, smiling triumphantly at her shock.

"Well," she said, as she grabbed a couple of cardboard boxes filled to the brim with microfilm reels, "You are a puny little thing aren't you? Are you sure you are getting enough vitamins?"

I frowned, wondering if she was somehow related to Alisa Mahn.

She guided me to where the projectors were, and instructed me on the basics of setting up, winding and rewinding prints.

"Okay, I'll be in the front, just holler if you need me," she said and left me to it.

I didn't even bother to look at the reels marked April and June – that had just been a ruse to conceal the month I was really after, just in case the woman tattled to Mariam.

"May 1989," I said, sliding the microfilm into the reader.

A couple of seconds later I was sliding through images of the Sand Point Times dilated on the screen in front of me.

May 15th, 16th…17th…18th… my heart skipped a beat. The day Yasmine's father had died. The day Yasmine had…changed.

What I needed was May 19th- the day after. Definitely, his death would have been reported…there might be an obituary or something…anything.

After several breathless moments of searching and struggling to wind the reel, I hit the jackpot.

My hands fell to my sides and my mouth dropped open.

There was a big headline in the Sand Point Times dated May 19th.

"LOCAL MAN FOUND DEAD AFTER MYSTERIOUS ROCKSLIDE".

Tillman's Gorge – The body of Sand Point resident, Sa'eed Ebrahim (35), was found at the foot of Tillman's Gorge by his wife and three other local residents.

Also discovered at the site, were two children, both aged 9 and one the daughter of the deceased. Both were in a state of shock but otherwise physically unharmed.

"It is indeed a mysterious thing," said Constable Roger Stone. "It is not possible for a rockslide to occur at this point of time when it is still too cold for the snow to melt."

The body had been discovered by the late resident's wife and local friends. "My daughter was supposed to have gone to her friend's place but when the friend's mother called to ask me about the girls, I realized something was amiss." Mariam Ebrahim, the wife of the deceased, told the police. "So, my husband offered to go look for both of them and when he didn't return, the friend's parents and I went looking for all of them."

She went on to say that after an hour of circling around unproductively, they stopped and asked a tuck shop owner if he had seen a blue Ford or two little children pass that way and he affirmed their suspicions and pointed to the road leading to the gorge.

Upon arriving at the scene, they found the car parked nearby and the missing little girls near an entrance to a small natural cave not too far away from the body of Sa'eed Ebrahim.

The little girls have not yet responded to questions asked about how and why they traipsed this far from home.

Forensics confirmed that the cause of death for Saeed Ebrahim was a fatal blow to the head by one of several heavy objects that matched the rocks lying near him. No foul play has been suspected.

There was no picture of her father and yet I could see him now.

Tall and broad with laughing hazel eyes, his big and gentle hands swinging me up and down while I screamed and gurgled in laughter.

Yasmine? I wondered, blinking. The memory I had seen was definitely through her eyes. Are you there? Are you awake? My heart beat faster as a dying hope was rekindled.

I felt something stir inside of me like it was trying to break through a fog, trying to wake up, trying to respond ...

I blinked through my tears. Yasmine, I thought. Yasmine, we need you honey. And not just me, Mama needs you, your family needs you! Wake up!

Everywhere around me was still and the only sound came from the gentle whirr of the desktop reader.

The silence continued for minutes that seemed to me like hours of loneliness and emptiness.

Yasmine... I said sorrowfully, throwing my plea out into the unsympathetic void, my shoulders sagging in disappointment.

And then she responded!

Like a sliver of white light illuminating the darkness, like a beacon of hope guiding sailors back to land, she responded!

Memory after memory rained down on me and I was too overwhelmed to sob with relief and joy.

Papa holding me tight, cooing and making baby noises...Mama taking photo after photo as I posed in my little cowgirl costume....Mama and Papa dancing together in the living room while Aboodi and I clapped and laughed along... Mama and Papa calling Aboodi and me to tell us news of relocating to Alaska...me nervously walking into my grade 1 class at Sandpoint Primary School and sitting beside a gap-toothed Samiya...

I was whirling around in a cornucopia of colourful, flamboyant memories, drinking in its spirit and its joy, like it was an elixir of life.

Yasmine, we are going to get to the bottom of this, I told her. Just hang on ok?

I felt her murmur in response, but that might have been my wishful thinking.

I carried the boxes of microfilm and was about to leave the room, when the door swung open inwards and I bumped into a flushed and panting Aboodi.

"Why, fancy meeting you here!" he growled, his eyes spitting fire. He grabbed me by the collar of my jacket and ignored the box of film crashing to the ground at our feet.

"Shouldn't you be at school?" I yelped.

"Shouldn't you be minding your own business?" he shot back, the veins in his forehead nearly popping.

He dragged me out of the room, across the faded carpet and dumped me on a seat farthest from the librarian's desk.

There was virtually no one around at that time and even the librarian was probably closeted somewhere having her lunch.

Aboodi sat across from me and held his head in his hands. "Isn't it enough for you that you got him killed and now you want to dig up his grave and stir up a hornet's nest?"

I winced. "What are you talking about?"

He looked up and I saw how tired his eyes were and how deep the dark circles ran. "About your current favourite topic, of course, what else?"

"Dad?" I asked.

"No, Brad Pitt!" he spat out and looked around him, but the library was still eerily quiet and void of any signs of life other than us.

"Well you and Mama had to be awfully stubborn about it, you left me no choice, see? I had to come here and find out for myself."

"What's there to find out?" he said. "You were the cause of everything, squirt, you led him to his death. You had to talk all high and mighty about your stupid imaginary friend and get him all worried and upset…"

My ears pricked up. "What? Come again?"

His upper lip curled in disgust. "Now act like you're all pancakes and dribbling honey! If you hadn't been so sick ever since Dad died, and if you weren't so puny. I would have boxed your ears for pretending!"

"Aboodi," I began, but he snubbed me off.

"He was so worried about you, he went to this lady witch-doctor, thinking you were seeing ghosts, did you ever know that?" he asked.

I shook my head, spellbound at the surprising turn of events.

"Who is this lady witch doctor?" I asked. "How did he find her?"

"He didn't," Aboodi said bitterly. "She found him. At about the exact same time he thought of looking for someone to enlighten him on your weird behaviour. Coincidence ya think?"

This didn't sound good, I thought.

"And it went downhill from there. Mama was getting upset when he reached home late or seemed distracted. She decided to follow him in a friend's car one day.

She saw him take the road to the deserted Tillman's Gorge and spend hours there inside a cave, she didn't see anybody else and this spooked her. Face it, man the whole place is known to be haunted!"

I was breathing hard, listening to every word with rising dread.

Aboodi's voice was shaking and he looked like he was going to cry.

"I remember him looking all anxious and so not himself. And you kept having these stupid tea parties with no body, having these stupid conversations with yourself and Dad would get all restless. You thought we didn't know about your little fairy friend, you thought you were keeping it a big secret, but really you gave Dad and Mom the heebie-jeebies."

"So why doesn't Mama talk about him anymore? Why did she throw away all our photos?"

"That's coz she thinks he cheated on her, dimwit! Even the day you went missing with that Mehmet kid, when all the grownups went searching for Dad after he had gone looking for you, it was on a hunch of hers that they went looking for him in Tillman's Gorge. And she was right. He was there."

"But the tuck shop owner..."

"Never existed," he said. "Mama invented an alibi, so she wouldn't have to drag Dad's name in the dirt by telling the Police how she came to think of looking for him in the gorge."

"But you don't honestly think she believes that he was seeing someone else do you?" I asked.

He snorted. "She used to ask him whose name he kept whispering in his sleep. She repeated that name several times to him, when I was around. It was an unusual name. It was all the proof Mama needed. I mean what other reason could be there for his disappearances and stuff?"

I chose to take that as a rhetoric question.

Aboodi laughed without mirth. "She totally lost it when I used to hang out for hours at the youth club. She thought I was also sneaking off to that death hole! As if I would! I've heard enough of that place to last me a lifetime without having to actually go there! Jeez! And now she's put me on a short leash! What have I ever done wrong, seriously, huh?"

"What was the unusual name of that woman?" I asked.

He frowned. "Why do you want to know? What does it concern you, squirt? I think I've told you enough as it is, mind you, not coz I think you're adult enough to hear it, but I was hoping the least you would do is stop picking on Mom about Dad. She's already hit a fuse, she might explode really."

"Yes, and I really appreciate all that you've told me, Aboodi," I said with feeling. "I also promise I won't bring it up in front of Mama again. But please tell me the name of that woman."

"Or what?" he challenged me.

"Or I'll ask Mama herself."

He screwed up his face in disapproval. "My, my, you give her a chocolate; she wants the whole box...you are a blackmailing little twat aren't you?"

"Aboodi, the name, please," and I let a slice of my real age creep into my voice.

It shook him slightly and he looked at me with a renewed attitude.

"Visa, I think, I can't recall." He stammered, still a little disoriented.

Vesta, I knew it. But what had she probed Yasmine's Dad for? Except for her first marriage, throughout the centuries she had never made contact with another human being. It had solely been my task to take hostage of human girls and their parents had never been directly involved. It was sort of a revenge turned hatred turned desperation on Vesta's part to indulge in such atrocity.

I stood up slowly and felt that here was yet another little mystery to be solved.

CHAPTER NINETEEN

That evening
1900 hrs

Aboodi was keeping an eye on me throughout. I guessed he felt I might go back on my word and try to badger Mariam for more information.

The truth was, I had received enough of information from him already and there was nothing else I could do without tearing an even bigger rift in the worn fabric of our family relationship. Two, I had made him a promise, and I would stick to it.

I was slowly stirring a big spoon through a red kidney bean salad while Mariam was sprinkling freshly ground pepper into a stock pot of creamy pasta.

Aboodi was stealthily throwing me anxious glares while he pretended to do his homework at the dining table. In the background, a deep voice was reciting a chapter of the Noble Book on one of Mariam's cassette players.

All in all, the cosiness of the room was shrouding a thick layer of disguised unease and mute apprehension, and that threatened to bubble over at the slightest prod.

"Mmm, yum, don't you think?" Mariam murmured; a gentle question, a simple lift of the spoon laden with creamy white pasta sauce, and the cauldron of tension wavered a little.

"Looks wonderful," I said blankly even though the aroma was quite enticing to my senses.

Mariam turned to smile softly at me before she extracted the spoon and replaced the lid of the pot. Switching off the stove, she untied her 'I LOVE BAKED ALASKA!' apron and took in a deep breath, and I was sure it was not the succulent food she was trying to get a whiff of.

"Smells like peace in here," she said, smiling.

Aboodi stared at me and I could picture him saying, "Is she getting high on pasta?!" or something of that sort. The cauldron of tension tilted backwards and the pressure within began to subside slowly.

I let out a small sigh of relief, glad that Mariam had more or less reverted to her usual self and was speaking to me like she had before the tiff had started.

"Ok, kids, why don't we do something creative while the pasta sets?" she asked suddenly, clasping her hands together in glee.

Aboodi looked to me again, his eyes wide in alarm, his pencil frozen over his math book. Mariam was not acting like herself, I wordlessly agreed with him.

"Something creative like what?" I asked at the same time as Aboodi said, "Are you sure you're alright, Mom?"

"Absolutely, Aboo, don't be silly," she said, frowning at him for a second before heading to the bookcase.

I shrugged at Aboodi behind Mariam's back, and took a seat at the table strewn with his books, papers and mathematical instruments.

"Here we go!" Mariam returned, carrying the thick volume of the Quran in her hands.

"Oh…" Aboodi rolled his eyes and threw his hands in the air. "It keeps playing in the back, nonstop already! Do we have to read from it too?"

"Abdallah, we made a pact to change ourselves!" Mariam glared at him as she cleared some space on the table to place the heavy book on it.

"No, Mom, you made a pact." He shot back.

"Abdallah!" she gritted her teeth and I could see the cauldron start to bubble once again.

The book landed with a thud on the table and it opened to a random page.

"I wish I had never strayed so far that my own children cannot embrace their own traditions!" Mariam sank into a chair and buried her face in her hands. Aboodi looked at me uneasily.

I leaned to the right and peeked at the opened chapter of the Quran.

The looping script once again beckoned to me in a voice I could not understand, in a language I found enigmatic and alluring.

"I am such a loser," Mariam sobbed, her shoulders heaving up and down, begging for consolation and forgiveness.

I did not grieve only for her sorrow but also for one that was more profound and ancient.

I had betrayed him. I had deceived him! How could I ever face him again?

An image of Al Barak floated in front of me and I saw his lips move slowly, beautifully, as he recited the divine words of God.

"Who is God?" I asked while the campfire between us danced and frolicked teasingly.

"God is Allah," He replied, the Holy Book lying open in his hands. "He is the creator of the universe, the all-knowing, the all-mighty and the one who needs no help. Look at the universe around you. Drink in its beauty and its complexity. Each part of the universe needs one another in order to ensure its existence and stability.

"Such a beautiful universe with its myriad little mechanics cannot come into existence without the design and sustenance of Allah the Almighty. Allah says..."

He lifted a palm and the pages of the book turned rapidly. "...in surah Anbiya – The Prophets – 'If there were in the heavens and the earth, other gods besides Allah, there would have been confusion in both! But glory be to Allah, the Lord of the Throne; (Far Exalted is He) above what they attribute to Him.'"

"But," I said, and he looked up. "Why does Lord Zeenon insist that we – our race- be worshipped? Is it all a hoax then? Why does he trick those humans?"

"Because he is merely following Darkness or Iblees himself instead of following the Light. Allah gave Iblees, the leader of the Jinn, respite till the Day of Reckoning. And Iblees vowed..." More

pages turned. "'By thy honour I shall certainly lead them astray, except those of thy servants whom Thou hast chosen.' This does not mean "I will not lead Your chosen servants astray," but instead: 'I shall have no power over your chosen servants.'"

I didn't say anything.

"Shaytaan or Iblees isn't our friend, little one, not ours, not theirs. He beguiles you with tales of grandeur, but they are all an illusion. Listen to this, Allah says in yet another Surah of his: 'And Shaytaan will say when the matter has been decided, 'Verily, Allah promised you a promise of truth. And I too promised you, but I betrayed you. I had no authority over you except that I called you, so you responded to me. So, blame me not, but blame yourselves. I cannot help you, nor can you help me. I deny your former act in associating with me (Shaitan) as a partner with Allah...'"

The recitation was breathtakingly beautiful and hauntingly sweet as always.

Before the meaning of the beautiful, striking words pierced my heart, its mesmerizing flow had already captivated my senses, leading me to believe, believe and BELIEVE in its very essence.

"'I have created jinns and men, that they may serve Me.'" quoted another follower in our little circle. "' No sustenance do I require of them nor do I require that they should feed me. For Allah is He who gives (all) sustenance, the Lord of Power, steadfast (Forever).'"

"Aah, the 51st chapter!" Al Barak smiled and only then did my slow mind realize that he had memorized the whole Book and my awe of him increased tenfold.

"Do you think that if He had not allowed it I would be able to do this?" Al Barak disappeared for a few seconds.

When he reappeared, he was smiling. "I had just visited India." He said.

"Or this?" he mutated into a bird and then back again.

"None of this would have been possible if my Lord Allah had deemed it impossible. Why do you think humans do not possess such powers? And yet they are more superior to us, Alhamdulilah- All praise to God!"

I was edging closer and closer to the light at the end of the tunnel. All I had to do was reach out and grasp the hand that was willing to take me into the light.

"Why am I not treated like the slave I'm supposed to be when I'm with all of you?" I asked, with wonder in my eyes.

He did not look directly at me out of bashfulness.

"Because in my eyes, you are not a slave," he answered. "Slavery was frowned upon by the last Messenger of God. And we don't believe in it anymore."

I was filled with gratitude and admiration and a longing to be one of the followers of the Light.

"How does one become a...a believer?" I asked.

Al Barak looked straight at me and his expression was hard to read. It was as if he was trying to control some inexplicable emotion.

He opened his mouth but at the same time there was a crack from somewhere.

"Akhi- brother- is somebody watching us?" a gasp came from within the circle.

Al Barak's eyes narrowed. "It could've been a forest creature," *he said but his eyes did not lose their cloud of suspicion.*

"It's about time we left, Maghrib is approaching. It's the Devil's playtime," one quiet female observed.

I gulped, taking the hit, even though I knew she would have never meant to direct it at me.

"Alright, everyone see you all tomorrow, Insha Allah-God willing!" *Al Barak smiled at me and looked away. "Stay safe, Ainee. We'll continue this tomorrow. Peace be upon you."*

I turned around and reluctantly thought of returning home to my degraded status. I didn't feel a pair of wicked eyes watch me from behind a prickly bush. I didn't realize then that I would be drawn back into the yawning darkness of the tunnel, saying goodbye to the rescuing hand forever.

CHAPTER TWENTY

The scene vanished, and Mariam's bent head flashed into focus. Time had stood still while I had revisited memory lane and filled in the little gaps with little exclamation marks and heart throbs.

Once again, I glanced at the opened page of the Quran. The words were still lost to me. I wondered if I would ever find them after choosing to shun them for three hundred years.

"Mar-Mom." I whispered. She didn't look up. Aboodi threw a question mark at me instead. I let out a huge breath and placed an unsteady hand on Mariam's still arm.

"Mama," I said again. "How do you find solace in this book?"

Aboodi snorted and Mariam finally looked up, her face red and her eyes streaming.

"Solace?" Aboodi said. "You won't find it in here; you'll find it in the dictionary!"

"Aboodi." I gave him a Look. Unsurprisingly, that quelled his jitteriness.

Mariam slowly closed the book and looked at me. "Why do you ask, Yasmine?"

I pulled out a chair next to her and sat down. "I dunno. I just wondered if you had committed deeds that you were not proud of. And you were afraid to turn to God for fear of His not accepting you."

Mariam sniffed and gave a watery smile to no one in particular. "Honey, surely what deeds have you done that you are afraid to turn to God and repent to Him?"

I heard the countless screams of generations of innocent girls echo in my head. "Nothing," I replied.

"Surely honey, you're still a child, I'm sure whatever it is you've done God surely wouldn't reproach you for it!"

I had turned away from the Light, in my weakness I had continued to do Darkness's bidding. I had three centuries to change but did not do so. Could not do so. Was that a viable explanation? Was I doomed for eternity? Oh surely, I had ruined thousands of lives, torn apart hundreds of families – how could I be sinless? How could I return to Goodness without some form of blackness tainting my soul?

And I was still writhing in the clutches of evil. I had probably committed the worst of acts by acquiring this child's body. Why had I even done so in the first place? How had I done so? How could I get out? How could I break free – from Yasmine, from Alaska, from Vesta-the whole world itself? I wished I had been born an ant instead. Or a blade of grass or even an atom. A short, straightforward, guiltless life.

"I guess He wouldn't," I replied, looking down at my feet.

Mariam brushed my hair back from my forehead. "Honey, whatever it is that is troubling you, I'll let you know that I returned to Allah. I chose to build a wall in front of the path I had treaded on earlier. Now I feel great and guided. I am not stumbling or even worse, blinded, anymore. What are we without Him, hon? If anything happens to us and we didn't 'believe', we wouldn't have a safety net to fall into. We wouldn't have hope in this life, we wouldn't feel calm in times of distress and I am beginning to realize this now. Seriously? I am beginning to wonder how I lived a lie all these years without seeking His guidance and support. Now I feel I can take on the world as long as He is there to Guide me."

She circled a hand around my shoulders and brought her nose to rub against mine. "Feel any better?"

No. I thought. It was easy for her to "revert", but my sins would make the Imam's nose fall off. "So, did you have to tell the Imam all your mistakes before you decided to change?"

She snorted, sounding just like her son. "Naw!" she said. "Whatever deed I do, good or bad, is between Allah and me. A good Muslim hides both his deeds from everyone else. You see, the special thing is you don't need a middle agent to direct your affairs to God. It's just you and God alone. Always. To Him, each of His creation is special! "

I pricked up my ears. "Really?"

"Really, really." She smiled. "So, whatever it is that has made you 'transgress all bounds', lovey, you just sort it out with Allah alone. You need not even tell me! Don't hold it back or let it restrain you from accepting the truth. Though I'm sure whatever it is, it's nothing Allah doesn't know about or wouldn't forgive. He is the Most Gracious, Most Merciful!"

Allah. The very name sent shivers running up my spine. I felt like I was a small speck being scrutinized under a microscope. If I was worried about betraying Al Barak, I was near hysteria wondering what the Supreme Lord of all Creation thought of me.

I felt exposed and this made me feel sick, suddenly. It was as if I was experiencing emotions that were too big for either body of mine to hold. I wished I had gone for one last meeting, so I could've found out what Al Barak had been trying to say before he was interrupted.

I was too afraid to pose the question now to Mariam – who was still a stranger to me despite her immense affection for the vessel I was harbouring. And the other thing was what would she feel if she knew this was not her daughter speaking to her? Would she still love me, or would she go ballistic?

I was also not sure I wanted to ask her. I was battling through conflicting sentiments where I alternated between crying out to Allah for help, and running away and hiding from the All Seeing, as futile as that sounded.

I realized I had never said 'Allah' in my entire life and I could not voice it now. I felt it would be a big crossover for me if I should say it and I was not ready.

"Are you alright?" Mariam placed a hand on my forehead. "You suddenly went pale."

I nodded weakly.

"Maybe her sins are weighing her down." Aboodi snickered from the opposite side, chewing on his pencil and throwing me a teasing look.

"Aboodi, one more remark and you will miss dinner!" Mariam said, without harshness.

"Aw, man!" he straightened up in his chair and bent over his long-neglected math homework.

"Mama, can I go upstairs?" I asked her.

"What, without dinner?" she looked aghast and disappointed.

"Save me heaps for breakfast," I tried to smile, already inching towards the staircase.

"Psst!" Aboodi called out in a mock whisper. "What do you mean by solace?"

"You'll find it in the dictionary," I winked at him and turned around to head upstairs, a smile on my lips.

CHAPTER TWENTY-ONE

Midnight

That night I dreamed.

I was in my white nightgown, my hair streaming in a thick cascade down my back. I was standing on my window ledge looking around at the quiet, moonlit nightscape.

There was a serene beauty kissing the gossamer moon threads that speckled every snow-clad object in its path.

As I stood on the top of my bedroom window ledge, two stories high, looking out at the still night, a soft wind caressed my face, and strangely it didn't feel cold or uncomfortable.

I felt I could fly and take on the world — my world- and bravely lifted a foot and stretched it out in the empty silvery air, when I felt a presence beside me, hovering just beside my window.

I looked around. At first I didn't see anything or anyone but then in the swirling mist, a dark shape began to materialize.

I opened my mouth to scream but it didn't come. Not this time.

"Hello, my angel." A voice as soft and slippery as the North wind ruffled every little hair on my body.

She was hovering just outside my window - a tall, thin, curvaceous woman with dark blue hair that swished to her waist and eyes that seemed to swallow her pointed face.

The child inside me stirred ever so slightly, and at the same time my unborn screams died within me.

I wanted to ask her who she was, but that question seemed unnecessary if not inappropriate. She was someone I had once known but forgotten. Now, looking at her, her identity was on the tip of my tongue but never coming to light.

Instead I chose to stare at her, my eyes overwhelmed with her ethereal beauty, my heart engulfed in a myriad of questions.

She smiled, and it was like the moon came out from behind a cloud. But it wasn't a luminous ebullient light that was emanating from her; it was more like the dark side of the moon smiling its sinister smile.

She held out her hand toward me, her fingers long and slightly curling, beckoning to me to join her, to trust her.

I hesitated. I wasn't sure what vibe I was picking up from her.

My left foot inched forward of its own accord.

She smiled again, and her hand continued to reach out to me invitingly. How could I refuse? My furiously throbbing heart went numb and my mind closed up.

Come, she sang. Her lips remained tilted in their maddening smile, but her words were echoing forth from a source other than her vocal chords.

Come to me, come with me... a sharp, melancholic song in a voice that was not of this world. It rang out from every part of her.

It pulled me gently, slowly, inevitably, towards the edge and I realized I was moving forward irrevocably and some of it was at my bidding.

She reached out with her other hand and I slowly held out mine in response, my mind choked in a trance, my faintly beating heart ensnared in her melody.

Come to me my beautiful child, come with me... let us share our dreams, our sorrows, our love....

The song went on and I dizzily felt my feet leave solid wood and tread on a cold cushion of air.

Here I am, words unknown to my conscious mind escaped through my parted lips as I held onto her hands for support and strength.

We continued to gaze into each other's eyes and motherly love poured endlessly from her eyes into my aching, lonely heart.

We shall be together, she whispered.

Forever and ever... I sighed on key.

Woooosh. The wind rustled to our words, creating a subtle harmony, as we flew through the air towards an unknown destination.

I didn't want this to end. I wanted this to go on forever and ever. I didn't know who I was nor did I care. The wind echoed my rapture and silent ecstasy.

But finally, after what seemed like the blink of an eye and simultaneously a three month's journey on a camel, we slowly descended to the ground.

At exactly the same moment that my bare feet hit the cold snow, my brain jerked awake and my heart jolted back to life.

I took a deep, painful breath and blinked.

"Welcome, my love!" her voice changed, and I saw my beautiful guide's features dissolve into that of an old, reptilian looking woman with sunken eye sockets, matted hair and a cruel leer. "Welcome to Tillman's Gorge, the place where it all began for you!"

"Vesta," I said, covering my ears to subdue not only my loudly convulsing heart, but also the shrill voice in my head that had begun to scream and scream and scream….

CHAPTER TWENTY-TWO

May 18th, 1989
Midnight

    My beautiful fairy pony landed as soft as a feather on the snow-caked ground, and I alighted from her back.
    "Ainee, that ride was awesome!" I said, "But I'm afraid Samiya's fainted or something. Can you help me get her down?"
    Ainee complied and slowly got down on her knees so I could pull, tug and yank my friend's heavy snoozing body off her back.
    I placed her as gently as I could on a slightly mossy patch of rock that hadn't been snow-drenched.
    She was snoring softly.
    I found that amusing. "Hey Ainee, do people snore when they have fainted or is it just coz she's fat?"
    My horse shook her magnificent black mane and blinked at me. I figured she didn't know either.
    Looking around, I noticed we were in a strange valley like place with the dying sunset obscured by a few jagged snowy, peaks in front of us.

There were trees around, heaps of them, and what looked like a little hole in the boulder in front of me. There were also remains of a fire.

"Ainee, where are we?" I asked her, hugging myself, for the wind had picked up a bit and this sent a chill running through me.

She trotted over to me and nuzzled my cold cheeks with her wet nose. It tickled me, but it also made me feel warm.

"So, what's this once in a life-time treasure you wanted me to see?" I whispered to her, as I put both arms around her.

I felt every sinew in her neck tense up and I wondered if it was because of my question.

But then, there was a crack of twigs and I turned around and saw a figure approaching us from the mouth of the cave.

"Hello, hello," said a woman's voice and the figure stepped into the waning light.

She looked exactly as my Ainee in her human form, except that she also looked older and …different. There was something about that difference in her that I couldn't decide, for it was not merely physical.

She held out both hands to me and curved her lips into a warm smile. I only tightened my grasp around Ainee's neck because I was beginning to feel cold again.

"Why, now, what's this hostility amongst friends?" she asked and then gasped. "Oh, wait, how silly of me, I didn't even introduce myself!"

She pranced forward and held out her hand. "I'm Vesta. But you can call me anything you like,"

I bit the insides of my cheeks and continued to stare at her. Ainee remained motionless underneath my embrace.

The woman – Vesta – withdrew her offer of friendship and looked at me studiously. Then her eyes wandered above my head and noticed the limp figure asleep on the rocks.

"Why, Ainee, you didn't tell me you were bringing over a guest as well!" she said, looking reproachfully at my Ainee.

With one long stride, Vesta reached Samiya's side, and I watched in trepidation as she bent over her and lifted a lock of her hair to peer at her face.

I didn't like the strange feeling that was creeping up my chest. Something wasn't right here. This place wasn't right. And I was sure Mama and Papa wouldn't approve of my being here in the company of…strange people.

I struggled to swallow a lump of fear while I gently stroked Ainee's silky soft mane. I wanted to tell her how scared I was and how small I felt but was afraid to open my mouth.

Ainee must have understood how I felt, for she nuzzled me again and whinnied softly to console me.

After a few troubled seconds, Vesta walked back to us. She looked a little disoriented and the spring in her step was gone.

Wordlessly, she waved her thick, dark cloak around and suddenly a fire roared at the mouth of the cave.

I took in a sharp breath and reminded myself that Ainee was magical so if Vesta was her friend, she might be possessing the same abilities too.

The blaze of the fire cast a golden halo against the blackening sky and its heat reached out to surround the whole perimeter of the gorge.

"Business now," the woman said, as she whipped out a copper kettle from nowhere and placed it on a hook above the fire.

Ainee flinched beside me and began trotting towards the woman and the fire.

I walked beside her, throwing back a glance to make sure Samiya was not left out of the encircling heat, and was relieved by the pink circles that were slowly spreading across her cheeks.

Ainee knelt on the ground and began to transform herself.

I sat cross-legged in front of the cackling fire and watched her become fluid air, as was her natural state.

"The treasure, Mother Vesta, as you requested," she said, and I could sense from her impassive tone that this was something she had said before too and was strangely not too happy about it.

I looked around, half expecting a treasure chest overflowing with gold coins and blazing rubies and emeralds, to materialize from nowhere, but I was disappointed.

"Yes..." Vesta said, and her voice sounded like a strange hiss. She began to crush some leaves and berries and throw them into the kettle over the fire.

"Well..." said Ainee and hovered in the air as if she were unsure and frightened.

I wanted to reach out and comfort her even though I myself was nearly collapsing from fear of the unknown. This isn't right, I thought. Ainee is so brave, so strong and so powerful. Why should she be afraid? And this thought only heightened my own state of anguish.

The woman began to hum a low, haunting tune under her breath as she stirred the contents of the kettle with a long wooden spoon. I heard a faint bubbling sound stem from it.

Ainee's form grew denser and her features merged into the face I loved and was familiar with – a young blue woman, an older sister, a mentoring friend.

She looked at me in concern and I could tell she was not happy at the sight of my trembling lips and questioning eyes. I was shivering now, and I wasn't sure if it was from the cold or from growing trepidation, even as I inched closer and closer to the fire.

"Slave!" said the woman behind the fire, and I looked up with a start, thinking she had addressed me, but Ainee stiffened and bowed her head in reply.

"I grow old and weary of this, of everything." The woman said, moaning slightly as she stirred the contents of the kettle. The bubbling sound amplified.

"I have kept my promise to Zeenon for so long, and what do I get in return? More pain. And worse than that, it repeats, and repeats and repeats and this cycle never ends!"

I gulped. The woman's voice had turned sour and her eyes were almost sunken in her head with despair. It was a garish sight.

Ainee was still bowing her head in silence.

I was beginning to lose control of my emotions. A strangled sob escaped from my lips as I thought of Papa and Mama safe at home probably assuming I was safe too at Samiya's place.

The creepy looking woman did not hear me. She was glaring at Ainee.

"My lady," said Ainee, not raising her chin. "I have brought you the child…"

The woman laughed and the malevolence in her tone rocketed around the valley and through the cold, forlorn night.

"Yes, my dear, obedient, stupid slave," the woman rasped, and her smile showed ugly, crooked teeth. "But even you do not know why you have brought me the child, do you?"

Ainee looked up and I saw surprise burst forth from her blue eyes.

"I beg to differ, my lady," she stammered, while she rubbed her fist with one nervous hand. "I have been doing this for quite a while now and I am certain..."

"...that you are unaware of the motive this time round." The woman finished, her eyes crinkling in a smile of self-satisfaction.

More dread welled up in my chest. I wished and wished that I was home safe in bed, with Mama bending over me to plant a goodnight kiss on my cheek.

Ainee's eyes were as wide as saucers. I could tell she was not in control of the situation anymore. My breathing was becoming more and more erratic as I watched the mounting tension in Ainee's form.

"For three hundred years and then some," the woman continued, rising to her feet, and I didn't know if it was because I was looking at her through leaping flames, but she appeared to have grown thinner and taller as if someone had stretched her like taffy. No traces of beauty remained on her face either.

"For three hundred years I was obedient to Zeenon. I did not go down and mingle with the flimsy humans. I thought my Alaira would leave behind a legacy once she passed on.

"She did. People began to worship our kind even more than before. They built statues in our honour, in shapes that we usually appeared and multiple temples were constructed in our name...Zeenon could not have been happier – his aim had been achieved.'

She bent to throw a branch into the fire and it hissed and snapped, demanding more.

"But, I don't see the purpose of it all. Now the intermingling of our kind with theirs is so common, you can't single out the incidents. You see people bowing down in shrines erected for the worship of our kind all over the world. It is so common that now they have forgotten who they are worshipping, they don't know anything about our race, they refer to us as 'ghosts' ,'spirits' or 'extra-terrestrial beings' whenever the most notorious of our kind mixes with them. PAH! Zeenon must be enjoying this little joke, but not me, not ME! I see no enjoyment in being unknown and unwanted. I want to LIVE again, I want to experience life, I want to hold my OWN child in my arms and I want to be FREE!"

She raised her hands up to the sky and screamed.

I clapped a hand over each ear and cried out from the shrillness of her voice.

"My Lady! My Lady!" Ainee tried to subdue her.

At last, when it seemed like her screams and my screams were one, and it would go on and on, she stopped.

The sudden silence was loud and fell on us like a cloak of relief.

I removed my hands from my ears and looked to Ainee with tears in my eyes. I wanted to get out of here, I wanted to leave NOW!

But Ainee was not looking in my direction. Her eyes were focused on the woman.

A strange, thin spire of grey smoke wafted up from the boiling kettle and snaked towards me. It tickled my nostrils and I smelt something sweet and pungent as well as black and foreboding.

"I decided this time, I wouldn't care," the woman continued, her head bowed, her voice constrained. "I decided if every low imbecile of our kind could do it, so could I. Let Zeenon rot in HELL!"

She threw back her head and laughed, an evil, agonizing, gurgling laugh that shook me to the core and chilled me to the bone yet again.

I tried to lean toward the fire for warmth, but the spicy odour from the kettle relentlessly jabbed at me, and I drew back, covering my nose and crying silently.

"My Lady," Ainee said. "Fighting fire with fire is not the answer. Why don't we…why shouldn't we…just a thought My Lady, why can't we switch tracks and seek Help from the Good…"

The woman took a deep breath and glared at Ainee and the latter shrunk back in fear.

"You think the forces of the Light will take me and YOU back after all the things we've done?! Do you honestly believe that you have any Good still left in you that they will welcome you with open arms? Will centuries of cradle-robbing suddenly disappear from your records? Pooh, child, you are a grown woman now and you still babble like a baby! The so-called GOOD was never meant for us! They refused us, they shunned us! And you want to go back to THEM?! That's worse than being Zeenon's pet mongrel."

"B..but My Lady…it's not like that, please, once we repent truthfully, we will be…"

"What, slave? We'll be what? Hugged and petted and kissed on either cheek? Blech! After sparing your worthless life from Zeenon's death grip, and feeding you and giving you companionship for eons, this is how you pay me back? By throwing hypocritical junk in my face?"

Ainee whimpered. I was crying openly even though I was not able to understand the extent of the conversation that was going on. My legs were starting to benumb from the cold, and the persistent fragrance kept forcing its way through my helpless nostrils.

"No, I know you, slave. I watched you attend those meetings with the other party." She floated towards Ainee and glared accusingly in her face.

"I saw how you looked at their fair leader and drank every word that he said like it was the only food you were being offered. I know what's in your heart. I know how weak you are…"

I saw Ainee tremble and shimmer into transparency before bouncing back to her present state.

"You think 'he' ever felt the same way about you as you did about him? Stupid girl! Just because 'they' don't believe in slavery doesn't mean they aren't biased! That's part of their scheme. Oh yes, they are scheming little devils too. Them and their Book. Do you know why you felt like swooning every time he would utter something from their Book? It was because it was full of spells! Spells to make you more submissive! Spells to make you turn your back on your own people! Goodness doesn't exist child! There's only evil. Evil, corruption, vice in everything and every place you go to…haven't you learnt anything in three hundred years?"

"But...but..." Ainee was shaking her head and I could see she was hurting. Hurting bad.

"Love is fruitless," the woman continued, circling Ainee's weak, trembling figure. "Where did it take me? I married and lost my husband, lost my child...I loved my brother and respected our Leader Zeenon, and what have I gained from it?"

She paused and lifted Ainee's hair from her forehead to peer into her downcast eyes. " I was given you...and after all these years of dutifully serving me, what do you say? 'Let's join the Good and be one happy family'..." her voice sank into a dangerous whisper and Ainee froze.

I froze too. But I guessed it was more to do with the numbness which had spread from my legs to my abdomen.

"But never mind," the woman smiled suddenly and the momentary pressure that had seized every floating molecule in the air, subsided.

She glided back to the fire, swinging her hips and tossing her long, frizzy blue hair over her shoulder.

"I have met someone...and he shall be my new partner. I may not love him, but I can use him. Use him as I have been used! He shall open the door to the life I have always wanted and only ever dreamed about. And this time there won't be anyone to stand in my way!"

She looked into the kettle bouncing merrily on the fire and her eyes literally glowed. She followed the streaming vapour and her eyes found me, half seated, half lying down in a state of semi-paralysis.

Just then the sound of screeching tyres broke into my cloudy brain.

The woman smiled, and her bestial features relaxed into the beautiful state I had first encountered her in.

"Aah, behold, Slave," she said, throwing her hands into the air. Her sharp talon like nails gleamed wickedly. "Here he comes now, just as I had envisioned! This is the very reason we came to Sand Point! It was for him, remember slave, the words that I utter now. It was for HIM that we came here. This year, we make history! My history!"

"B..but the girl...you wanted me to watch the girl for the last two years..." Ainee's voice echoed from far away, like the other end of a long, dark tunnel.

I woozily sank further into the ground, my eyes fighting to stay awake.

The woman snickered, and I heard footsteps pounding, heading our way. "The girl was just bait, Slave. You were to use her to get the father to come to me...everything worked according to plan! And tonight, he comes for me!"

"But how...why...when did you change your mind? This is the correct time for a descendant of your progeny to return to you...I assumed..."

"The child is still here, slave. The child that would've come to us had I not decided to switch tracks. But it is not the child of the father who will appear before our eyes in a few seconds. Ironically, you brought her to me too, even though I gave up on the idea. Sometimes slave, your stupidity can be mistaken for a sense of humour!

"The chosen or rather recently un-chosen child is that vain, selfish little dumpling, snoring in the corner – Samiya."

CHAPTER TWENTY-THREE

May 18th, 1989
Continued

The scene ended with a flash and was immediately replaced with a new one. But this time the angle was different and the eyes through which I was viewing the memory were my own.

I was floating in mid-air to the far right of the fire and the partially hidden cave, whilst the sprawling form of Yasmine was several feet to my left.

Suddenly there was a rustle and a pant and the sound of heavy footsteps brought a newcomer into the zone.
I quickly blinked into invisibility.

"Aaah – Sa'eed! Welcome," Vesta, the evil witch, held out her arms towards him, the sleeves of her dark robe almost drooping to the ground.

He was a tall, well-structured man in his mid-thirties, and even his distress could not deny his good looks. He was panting, and it was not from the exertion of climbing up the steep path to the gorge.

"Vesta..." he began fiercely, and then his eyes fell on the limp bundle of his daughter, curled into a fetal position on the cold ground before him.

"Oh my God!" he thundered and skidded to where she lay. "Yasmine, Yasmine, wake up!"

"She's only asleep, dear," Vesta crooned, while she calmly watched the man frantically trying to rouse his daughter to consciousness.

"Yasmine!!!"

"Sa'eed, darling, I had to bring her here you see, but I would not harm her. I just had to make sure you would come to me just like you promised."

He looked up to her and his eyes were brimming with tears. "What have you done to her?" he said in a choked voice.

I observed that Vesta was losing her cool. "Sa'eed," she said, and her voice took on a stronger definition.

He was unable to resist her invisible charm. His head jerked up to face her, even though his trembling hands were tenderly cradling his daughter's head in his lap.

She smiled, probably hoping that it would soften the edges of her previous remark, but he didn't look mollified.

Stepping around the fire towards him, she began to hum her haunting little ballad.

Come to me, my precious one, come with me...

The kettle swinging over the flames continued to cast its soporific fumes endlessly.

I watched helplessly as the man's hands relaxed their hold on his daughter's head, and his eyes slowly shifted out of focus.

"Sa'eed, tonight will you become my husband?" Vesta whispered in his ear.

The flames cackled and spat. The kettle churned and rattled. Even though the spell didn't work on me, I was petrified, torn between an earnest desperation to do something and a hopeless dread that if I did, the situation would only worsen.

He blinked blearily at her. "Mariam…" he murmured.

Vesta gritted her teeth and glared in his face. "Sa'eed…" she cajoled in a sing song voice as if he were a little child. "You are beginning to test my patience! Now. Will. You. Marry. Me!"

"Mariam, Mariam…" he chanted.

With a snarl of rage, Vesta drew her hand back and slapped him with full force across his face.

He flew several feet, straight into the side of a rocky outer wall of the cave and crashed into it.

"You incompetent fool!" Vesta bellowed and rose to a majestic seven feet in height, her facial features morphing in accordance.

I blinked out and reappeared in visible form at Yasmine's side. "Yasmine," I whispered urgently. She was stone cold, and the little bit of colour left on her cheeks was beginning to recede too. I smoothed the soft brown tendrils of hair off her forehead.

"You came to me for help, I soothed your worries, I gave you comfort that your nagging wife never gave you!" the confrontation continued.

He was slowly clambering out of his hypnotic daze now that he was away from the noxious fumes of the fire.

"My wife never nagged me," he sputtered, his eyes resuming their natural colour. "She was just edgy about the whole Alaska shift."

"And your daughter?" Vesta leered. "The visions she kept having and the conversations with 'ghosts'...did your beloved Mariam listen to your worries? Did she suggest that they might not be the little girl's imagination after all? Did I not offer you the answers you needed?"

"Yes," he said, and anger crept into his tone. "But you dragged me into a world I would have preferred not to have known."

"Why, does our kind scare you?" she sneaked towards him, her tone taunting.

He looked at her now unattractive features and inhuman figure and did not quail at the peculiar sight.

"How do I know that all of this isn't part of a hidden agenda of yours, Vesta?" he said, climbing to his feet. "How can I be certain that you are not the very reason my daughter fell into jeopardy? I mean, you are one of them! And you claim she is being visited by one of them! And where did you suddenly appear from, just at the right moment when I was searching for answers? If you ask me, Vesta, I should be running away from you and not towards you. I have been a total idiot!"

He rubbed the back of his sore head and glared at her. She glared back, and the strong emotions sizzling between them were almost tangible.

"Yasmine!" I begged the little girl to wake up. She didn't budge. Her face was slowly turning blue as the fumes had taken a strong hold on her.

I closed my eyes and concentrated on the solid form of a black Rottweiler.

I felt myself expand and harden and when I was down on all fours, I leapt over the flames in one bound and knocked the poisonous apparatus to the ground.

Yasmine - I turned towards her and nudged her face with my jaw and licked her unyielding cheeks with my warm, wet tongue.

"Why did you promise you would come tonight?" Vesta asked, and the hills echoed with her fury and pent-up pain

"Months of your drugged tea made me pronounce sentiments I am now ashamed to recall," Sa'eed said.

"You said you found me fascinating!" she said, and her voice shook a little.

"I think 'different' was the word I'd used."

"You…why did you say that you would come tonight?" she repeated and shrunk to her previous modest size, but her eyes were huge and filed with a demented longing.

Sa'eed looked down at her and his jaw hardened. "I thought I would use the opportunity to say farewell. My wife, my children, my whole life is falling apart and spending time with you is only aggravating the condition. I should have never believed you would help me. There's only one person who can help me and I should have turned to Him earlier. Way, way earlier. I had jumped from the chopping board into the frying pan. And now I WILL not jump into the fire! I have wronged my soul enough! Goodbye Vesta."

He pushed past her and limped towards Yasmine.

That was when he saw the big Rottweiler licking his beloved daughter's face.

"You!" he roared, pointing a finger at me and somehow I guessed he knew my identity. His eyes flashed with blame, distress and anger.

"Get away from my baby, y'hear?!" he gritted his teeth and advanced towards me menacingly.

I crouched low, whimpering in remorse. I love her too, I silently pleaded to him. I don't want her to die either! I am not her enemy!

"You've done enough of damage, you mongrel!" he said, unyielding to my beseeching eyes.

And in my mind I was hearing Zeenon's voice all over again. But Yasmine's Dad is good, I thought. He is not like Zeenon. He is not a cruel person. He just loved his daughter and was assuming I was trying to harm her.

And wasn't he right? Hadn't I been trying to harm her? I had befriended this little girl with the ultimate goal of bringing her to her doom and was now trying ardently to save her. Who was I? What kind of a beast was I?

There is no good, I remembered Vesta saying. There is only evil. Goodness is just a disguise that evil sometimes cloaks itself in.

I whimpered again.

"Sa'eed."- A stentorian command like the crack of a whip and he turned around.

Vesta was looking at him with eyes that were once again sunken in so deep they resembled twin galleons floating in their own wretched orbits.

"For three hundred years I have waited. And finally, when I achieved what my heart desired, I am still facing obstacles!" she growled.

He didn't flinch. "I said goodbye, Vesta." He turned towards me again.

That was when he saw the second supine figure lying on the ground, just outside the diminishing light of the fire.

"What on earth…" he squinted but wasn't given a chance to complete his sentence.

A brutal roar filled the air and he was flung backwards for the second time against the rocky wall.

"I WON'T LET A WEAK HUMAN TAKE CONTROL OF MY WISHES!" Vesta bellowed.

This time Sa'eed was hurt more severely. He coughed up blood and struggled to get to his feet.

She stooped beside him and raised his chin to glare into his adamant eyes.

"Tell me, worthless human, before you die, who is that one person you would have taken for your protector other than me?"

He wheezed and struggled for breath, but his eyes never gave in to her wrathful gaze.

"He is Allah, the One! Allah, the Eternal, Absolute! He begets not, nor is He begotten. And there is NONE comparable unto Him!"

A spasm shook my body. I felt Samiya slowly stir to consciousness to my left. And Vesta – Vesta lost control.

"You…VERMIN!" she raised her arms and there was a noise like a peal of thunder or the sound of a thousand hooves thundering in the sky.

The hills around us began to tremble as if they were awakening from a deep slumber. One by one, huge boulders began to loosen and roll down. The earth shook, and the night shuddered and gasped.

"Any last words, slime?" Vesta spat out, her eyes glowing orange.

Sa'eed looked up at the approaching disaster with tears in his eyes. But they weren't tears of fear for his imminent death.

"O Allah, forgive me! Protect my family!" he croaked, clasping his bloodied hands together and raising his face to the thundering sky. "Ash-hadu an laa ilaha Illallah waashadu anna muhammadur rasoolullah! I bear witness that there is no God worthy of worship but Allah and Muhammad is the messenger of Allah…"

I yelped and buried my stinging face in Yasmine's thick jacket. All around me rocks were raining down. I tugged at Yasmine's jacket with my teeth and dragged her heavy, uncompromising form towards where Samiya lay, stirring from her long sleep.

When the two girls lay together, side by side, I draped my body over them, shielding them from any harm.

Suddenly a shadow loomed over me and I opened my yellow eyes to glower at Vesta's brooding presence.

"Your little friend is all but dead, my hypocritical slave," she bent towards me and whispered in my ears. Her eyes gleamed with madness. Something had definitely snapped in her. "How are you going to save her now? Where is the good you keep bragging about? Didn't I tell you everything is a sham? First the father, now his daughter. Say goodbye to her, slave."

I was weeping endlessly inside, even though my canine features remained impassive. The grief I had felt over and over for *betraying Al Barak had now resurfaced in the form of letting little Yasmine down.*

Good does exist, Vesta. I said. I'm sure you're wrong.

And I did the one thing that I thought would save Yasmine's life.

When Samiya was fully awake a full five minutes later, the rescue party had just arrived and was exclaiming over her and an unconscious but stable Yasmine, and the death of Sa'eed Ebrahim was listed in the following day's newspaper as a fatality.

CHAPTER TWENTY-FOUR

The present
February 23rd, 1992
Saturday
0045 hrs

The final vision ended. My memories had returned to me and I was myself once again.

The big problem was that I was still trapped inside the body of a twelve-year-old with no clue of escaping. Then there was the other little issue of my current location.

I looked around me.

Tillman's Gorge had somewhat shrunk since the last time I had been there, maybe because of the massive rockslide that had choked up most of the area.

The cave was no longer to be seen but the evil woman was bending over a fire a few feet ahead of me, and the déjà vu wasn't a pleasant one.

She looked up at me, her face once again assuming its beautiful version.

"Finally finished with your little day dreaming, dear?" she asked, stifling a mock yawn. "I thought I'd be stuck here for another couple hundred years…"

"Why are you still alive?" I interrupted, surprising even myself with my wantonness.

"I should be asking you that very question." she said, smiling serenely, as she examined her cuticles.

I raised an eyebrow. The wind picked up a bit and whipped through my nightgown, making it swirl against my ankles, but I didn't feel cold at all. I realized that I didn't feel anything for that matter.

"Why did you bring me – us here, Vesta? You don't need this child. And the man is dead. Why can't you leave them be?"

She leaned into the fire and looked up at me, and the reflection of the flames danced mischievously in her eyes.

"Ainee." she said and I realized that this was the first time in our lives she had called me by my name. The rhythm of my name on her tongue sounded ominous and alien to my ears.

"I brought you here to warn you." she smiled softly, threateningly. "The child you are harbouring is close to death. You have been crushing her life force slowly, for the past three years, even though in the beginning your strength helped save her waning life. And she will finally give in very, very soon. I'm afraid you have no time left."

"What's your point, Vesta?" I asked valiantly, even though her words had shaken me up inside.

"My point, is," she leaned back and away from the fire so that her eyes were no longer dancing fireballs. "My point is, once that child dies, you will automatically be liberated, and once you are, you will return as my slave. And I swear to you. This time I will personally hand you over to Zeenon and I will watch as he pummels you to your death. You know what? I look forward to that!"

"Why would you even think of joining forces with Zeenon? You chose to betray him three years ago! Surely he would know of that!"

"No, that's where you are wrong, my dear." Her voice was milk and honey. "And what Zeenon doesn't know cannot harm me!"

I gulped and balled my little hands into fists.

"I am not afraid to die," I said, my voice coming out tinny and girlish. "But I'd rather spare Yasmine's life. How much time do I have till she…till she fades away?"

Vesta curled her lips up in a crooked grin, both beautiful and grotesque at the same time.

"Till tomorrow." she announced.

"You lie!" I shouted out, taking an impulsive step backward.

"Well, you can sit and wait it out and see for yourself," she shrugged teasingly. "Or you can try to get out and spare at least one life."

"How do I get out?" I stammered, hating myself for having to beg her for an answer, and also knowing the chances of her giving it to me were slim to none.

"Well, well, well," and she laughed with humour. "Isn't it ironic, the very weapon you thought you'd use to save a life would also crush it to death? A double-edged sword, surely!"

I bit my tongue, trying not to let my panic break through its barriers.

"Vesta..!" a strangled cry escaped from my lips and she only laughed louder.

"Not so cocky anymore, are we?" she mocked me.

I looked around, appealing to every particle of snow and every fibre of rock in the vicinity to help me out.

Vesta laughed and laughed and the loud, cruel sound drowned the stillness of the night.

"Tomorrow, same time, same place, Lord Zeenon will be here to personally see to your own burial." She said suddenly, all seriousness back in her tone.

I hugged my quaking body in response.

She rose to her feet, turning around, before she stopped suddenly and looked back at me.

"Oh, and I've changed my mind about something. Tomorrow I am going to grab that Mehmet girl. I've decided to restart collecting little dolls but for a different, uncanny hobby I have thought of. Want to hear all about it?"

My ears pricked up. "No," I whispered.

She smiled back, and to an untrained eye it would have appeared that she was trying to comfort me like a mother would comfort her little daughter.

"I know she is a tad too old for my liking and since she has already crossed over the border between childhood and womanhood, she won't adapt to our clandestine lives like her ancestors did, but her struggles will make it all the more appeasing for me! I have renounced trying to love little brats when all they could do was whine and pass out on me. This new pastime of mine will open new horizons and I'm so sure Zeenon would approve. Ta-ta!"

With a wave of her cloak, she and the fire disappeared in the blink of an eye and I was left in the cold, dark and empty valley, shivering from pure agony and grief.

"Oh no! Oh no! Yasmine! Yasmine!" I sank to the floor and burst into dry sobs. "Yasmine! Yasmine!"

I screamed out her name several times but she didn't reply.

"Yasmine, what have I done! Yasmine! Yasmine!"

And then someone spoke back to me.

"What kind of a devil are you!"

I gasped and turned around and found myself staring into the fuming face of Aboodi!

In my near hysteria, his name failed to enter my mind and I just gibbered out of shock and relief.

"I followed you." he shut me up, and I saw that his eyes looked haunted and his skin was pale. "I heard a noise from your room. It was like the other night when you tried to walk through the window. At first I ignored the noise, thinking it might've been a rat, but then I looked out of my window and saw you...saw you *float out of your window!!* I tiptoed out of the house without waking Mom up and followed you all the way here. Who was that woman? Why did she bring you here? And…and who are you? You aren't my sister are you?"

He looked frightened and sceptical, and it was then that I realized I had found a wonderful ally in the form of Yasmine's older, self-obsessed brother.

"I will tell you my story on the way home," I promised him, my dying resolve rising with a much-needed burst of hope.

CHAPTER TWENTY-FIVE

Saturday
0200 hrs

We reached home finally, after walking all the way from the ill-famed place we were grateful to leave behind. Aboodi was shivering in the thick coat and hat he had hurriedly draped over his pajamas and I was not feeling the cold at all as I walked by his side, in nothing more than a long, barely-warm nightgown.

I started my story at the very beginning , from my slavery to Zeenon and by the time we reached our front door, I had finished the entire sordid tale.

Both of us paused at the front stoop, and I turned to study Aboodi's face in the pale moonlight.

He deserved a gold medal for not screaming or losing his cool throughout the hike home. My story was not a bedtime fairy tale nor did it come close to an eighteen plus rating.

But throughout my speech, he had not said a word, and his sharp features had remained impassive and stone-like.

"Well," I said. "Will you help me?"

He did not look at me, but chose to stare at the door instead.

"I dunno what to say," he said expressionlessly, after clearing his throat.

I sighed, taking in his striking half boy- half man features and for the first time, appreciated his courage and strength in the face of an inexplicable situation. He was his father's son through and through.

"Aboodi," I reached out and placed a shaky hand on his sleeve.

He jerked back as if he had been struck by lightning.

"D-don't touch me, 'kay?" he said, finally glaring at me with eyes that betrayed his youth and the fear he was holding inside.

"I will not hurt you, Aboodi." I said, pained.

"You are some strange sort of creature choking the life out of my lil sis..." he responded, and his voice broke, even though his tone was forceful.

"Yes, but I want out! I want to save your sister. I am one of the good guys, Aboodi!" I insisted.

His breath came out in little white mists. "I don't think you know what 'good' means," he said, his words aiming straight for my heart. "If you had, you would have never returned to your master! You would have joined the good guys. You would have asked them to help you! All this would never have happened! My Dad would have never died!"

I pursed my lips in agitation. "It isn't easy as you think it is, Abood-"

"Abdallah!" he shouted back. "My name is Abdallah! And if you want to know what difficulty is, try putting yourself in my place now and imagine that the sister you have been living with for the past three years is not the same person you thought she was! How's that for not easy? And wait- this is just the tip of the ice berg!"

I bowed my head, unable to reply, while he exhaled loudly and stormily in front of me.

"I'm going inside," he said, after a few minutes of heavy silence. "No point hanging around here trying to catch hypothermia."

He made to open the door, when I reached a tentative hand and stopped him.

"Please, not a word to Mariam," I begged him, my eyes wide with fervour. "Not for the moment at least."

Suddenly we had switched places on the court and now I was the one worried about him prattling to Mariam. He seemed to realize this and his eyes twitched ever so slightly.

"We shall continue this tomorrow morning," he said gruffly. "Right now, I'm tired as hell and wanna sleep. And hopefully by tomorrow I'll realize that all of this has just been one crazy dream!"

I nodded in gratitude, sensing a truce, and snatched hopefully at the hint of reconciliation that had sprung up.

Tomorrow was going to be another nightmare.

CHAPTER TWENTY-SIX

Saturday
0900 hrs

Mariam had left early to do some grocery shopping; the note on the refrigerator confirmed that.

I had not slept at all the previous night. My mind had been my own personal whirlpool of churning, turbulent thoughts, that I had not been able to have forty winks. However, the opposite could be said of Yasmine.

If what the evil crone had professed was true, then Yasmine's time was ticking and she was not showing any inclination to wake up before she was forced to say goodbye.

And I had not crept one bit closer to discovering how I could save her life, or mine for that matter.

I just sat at the dining table for over an hour, staring at the empty scratched top, my mind milked dry, my heart void of any emotion.

Suddenly, thudding footsteps could be heard from upstairs, and soon, Aboodi came jogging down dressed in his joggers, bleary eyed, pale-faced but wide-awake.

"Mornin'." He nodded, smiling, before heading to the refrigerator to pull out a carton of milk.

"Mornin'," I replied, dubious of his semi-cheerful tone especially after last night's abrupt parting.

He seemed to sense my eyes boring into him and turned to me, a clean glass in hand. "What?"

"What?" I stared back.

He poured himself some milk, replaced the half-empty carton, and pulled a chair backwards to sit opposite from me.

"Y'know, I had a weird dream last night…" he said, grinning slightly.

I rolled my eyes in silent frustration. "Aboo…Abdallah! It wasn't a dream. It was very much real!"

The smile froze on his face. "You've GOT to be kidding me!"

I gritted my teeth and sighed. "Tillman's Gorge…weird lady…flying through the air…possessed little sister…hell, yeah! It all happened!"

He stared at me and the glass of milk was slowly lowered to the table, un-drunk and no longer a priority.

The staring match continued for a while and I was sure he was cataloguing a lot of the moments he had experienced last night, while my intent look was one of judgmental observation.

"What do we do?" he finally appealed to me, as his shoulders sagged and his eyes dimmed.

"I dunno," I replied. "My priority is your sister's life. I need to get out of her ASAP."

"So, the reason she's so small and malnourished is coz you are in her?" he asked simply.

I didn't reply but my expression was affirmation enough.

He shook his head and clicked his tongue in what appeared to be a resurrection of his previous fury, but all he said was, "I should hate you with all my heart, but I can't find it in me to detest a creature who is so helpless herself."

Something in me softened and I realized here was someone who wasn't the self-centred, arrogant boar that I thought he was.

"So, your name is Ainee?" he asked.

"Yeah,"

"What's that mean?"

"Well," I said, stealing a furtive glance at the relentless clock. "It's an old name. In Arabic it means 'My eyes'. In Irish Gaelic it's derived from the word 'Aine' when simply put, means ardent. Whereas in Celtic, it means fire or joy."

He nodded. "So what are you, an alien or a fallen angel? What is your species?"

"We are just another creation of God." I said, parroting verses from the happiest, short-lived part of my life. "Man was created from sounding clay, angels from light and we were created from a subtle or an elemental fire. Man cannot see us unless we choose to show ourselves, by shape-shifting into a creature familiar to man. However, we have been commanded not to, and to keep to ourselves. Sadly, most of us pay no heed to it and thus dig our own graves, myself included."

"Wow!" Aboodi said, totally ignoring the sudden sadness evident in my voice. "You guys can shape-shift?"

"Uh-huh,"

"Awesome, man! Like, that's totally crazy! Are you sure you're not kidding me?" He was practically jumping up in elation.

And I was reminded that he was still mostly child than adult, despite his mature physical appearance, and that he was tackling trauma on a very high level.

"Abdallah," I said, trying to inject a hint of sternness in my tone to bring him down to earth. "The very reason you are here having this peculiar conversation with me was because I went astray and shape-shifted to lure an innocent mortal girl to danger, year after year, century after century. This is not a lighthearted matter! It is very serious!"

He sighed, but struggled to maintain a straight face. "I sure wish Mom would believe us if we told her about this! But adults are no fun. I'm sure she would think I'd gone loony or something!" Then his eyes widened and he clicked his fingers. "Light bulb!! Hey, maybe you could prove to her that I'm not making this up! You could morph in front of her eyes and show her who you really are! Just wield your magic powers. Ka-zam!"

This time I didn't hide my desperate glance toward the clock. It was half past nine.

"Abdallah," I began.

"Aboodi!" he corrected me, flashing a wide, cheesy grin. "Forget what I said last night. Had I known you had the power to burn me to cinders with your bionic laser vision, I wouldn't have acted all tough-guy on you!"

I pressed my tongue to my cheek, not knowing whether to laugh or cry. This situation was getting beyond psychotic.

"Abdallah," I repeated and his wide grin wavered a little. "Sorry to disappoint you, but I don't have laser vision, and I will not morph to entertain your mother. If she knew who I was, she wouldn't waste a second trying to kill me with her bare hands. Besides, we should be concentrating on the apocalyptic circumstances at hand here. There is too much at risk."

His mouth lolled open. "Apollo wha-?"

"Apocalyptic – disastrous, end of times…never mind, three lives at stake here…"

"Three?" he repeated dazedly, and I figured the excitement had receded into a shock that had numbed his brain.

"Yes," I said, reaching for the phone. "And this does not count yours or Mariam's. I just remembered Alisa Mahn's party is this evening, and we don't want Samiya sneaking out of home tonight of all nights. It'll be like walking into the brunt of a storm."

CHAPTER TWENTY-SEVEN

"Hello," Samiya picked up the phone.

"Hey, Samiya..." my voice trailed uncertainly.

"Yasmine?" she sounded surprised, miffed, uncertain.

"Yeah, hey, what are you up to? How's school going? Anyone miss me while I'm here counting the spots on my ceiling?"

"Yasmine, I gotta go now, Mom's calling me..." Her voice reeked with guilt.

"Listen, Samiya," I said, throwing all caution to the wind. "You can't go to Alisa Mahn's party. It's too dangerous! It's a matter of life and death! I'm not kidding!"

There was a sharp intake of breath and I could visualize her checking over her shoulder to make sure no one was around.

"Yasmine!" she hissed close to the mouthpiece, her voice low and angry. "How dare you! How dare you have the nerve to call me at my house and tell me not to go to a party I was invited to? This is so low of you, Yasmine! I didn't know you had it in you to be so awfully jealous!"

I actually stamped my foot in exasperation. "No! You've got it all wrong! I'm not jealous! I'm trying to look out for you! You should not leave home tonight! Just stay close to your parents...don't even think about sleeping in your own room!"

"Yasmine? Chill. You're obviously sick. You need medication." Oh great, the Alisa Mahn virus had gotten to her too. "I am going to this party whether you like it or not, and if you try to call me again or snitch on me, I swear, when you come back to school next week, you'll wish that everyone just ignored you like before."

"Samiya..."

"Goodbye, Yasmine. Just forget I was ever your friend!" The line went dead.

❄ ❄ ❄

"I take it things didn't go too well," Aboodi said, as I dejectedly placed the receiver back in its cradle.

"I think I just made things worse," I muttered, turning around to face him.

He didn't say anything.

"Guess we'll have to personally stalk her house and make sure she doesn't leave it, around six pm." I said, rubbing my throbbing forehead.

"But, we can't leave the house, remember? We're grounded. And with both of us gone at the same time, Mom's bound to notice!"

I swallowed. "I'll do it on my own then, while you keep her distracted. There's no point getting you exposed to the Vesta allegiance anyway."

"No," he said and a glimpse of his maturity of last night peeked in. "I'm way too deep in this to back out. Wherever you go, I go too."

"Abdallah..." I began, sighing.

"Aboodi!" he insisted.

"YEAH! ALRIGHT! ABOODI!" I yelled. "Aboodi! This isn't a game, alright? It's not some adventure that you watch on TV or read in a mystery novel. This is real life to the core. If you get hurt, or die, there are no second chances! There is no reload button! This battlefield, kid, is the real goods."

He stood up and tall. His gaze didn't falter. "I'm still in." he said, emphasizing every word.

"Aboodi," my voice broke a little as I momentarily saw Sa'eed stand in his place. "I am responsible for your father's death and if things go bad, your sister's too. Please don't add any more casualties to the list!"

He locked his jaw and barrelled his hundred-pound stare at me.

I pursed my lips. "What? Are you trying to burn me to cinders with your bionic laser vision?"

I thought he would burst out laughing or maybe snicker a little in his usual way, but all he did was swallow. His eyes misted a little and he said. "I don't want my father's death to be in vain. I will fight the monster behind all of this or die trying."

I leaned forward and hugged him tight.

"Aboodi," I said, concentrating on squeezing my eyes shut to avoid breaking down completely. "These are my people we are talking about. You are no match for them. I don't want you to unnecessarily do anything that would endanger your life. Bravery is one thing, and I am so grateful and proud of you for it, but foolishness is another. And fighting these people is way beyond possibility, unless you are foolish enough to risk it."

He pushed me back and looked away. "Why are you against telling Mom? She could help."

"How?"

"I dunno…she's an adult." He looked at me and shrugged like it was obvious.

"So am I, kid, even though I'm stuck in this child's body. And I'm stronger than your Mom too at that. And still that's not enough."

"What about the Imam then?" he asked suddenly.

"What about him?"

"Well, maybe he could help out with um…freeing you…"

"What?! How?!" I reeled back in shock.

"Haven't you heard of exorcism?" Aboodi asked in surprise.

Exorcism- a ceremony to drive out evil spirits believed to possess a person or place.

"You've been watching too many horror movies."

But he wasn't ready to abandon what he thought was a 'eureka' moment of his.

"Not too many movies. Just one actually. It was called The Exorcist. I watched it at my buddy Ryan's place last month. It's about this girl who's possessed by this ghost..."

"Yeah, yeah, ok," I said, shuddering. "Skip to the facts, kid. Firstly, there is no such thing as ghosts. It's only this fabricated story that one of our descendants, Alaira had helped pass around to hoodwink humans. You should read up on Jinns to find out more about our surreptitious antics. Secondly, what makes you think the Imam is capable of conducting an exorcism?"

"Well," he shrugged again, slightly vexed that I hadn't taken to his plan as he had hoped I would. "He is the leader of our community. He should be very knowledgeable. If you say that your kind is mentioned in the Quran, then he should be well versed about your characteristics. We could just go up to him and ask him to help free you out. Maybe there are some Quranic verses that make this possible."

I was dubious about the entire procedure. And petrified that I would face the same phenomenon that I had undergone at Persepolis when Al Barak and his clan had opened their mouths to wound us.

Then I remembered the Imam's piercing gaze at Mama's lunch, and also his desire for me to listen to the recitation of the Quran. Did he already suspect that something was not right here? If he had, why had he not mentioned it to Mariam?

"Don't we have any other option?" I asked.

Aboodi shook his head. "None. Unless you want to wait till tonight when you are automatically set free..."

He let his voice trail but a dark look stole into his eyes. It reminded me that the momentary respite in our rickety relationship had risen only because of my willingness to free his sister.

At the end of the day, blood is still thicker than water, and he wouldn't have been sitting here plotting with me companionably, if I hadn't shown an inclination to reverse the calamitous scenario that was looming ahead.

"Ok." I said. "How do we go to him?"

He straightened up. "We ride our bikes to his lodge. It's only a kilometre from here and in the melting snow, we can reach there within half an hour."

"So, what's your strategy?" I asked, my fingers tapping nervously on the sideboard.

"Just tell him point blank is all," he said. "Ask him if he knows how to free you coz Yasmine's only got a few more hours to live."

"Ok. But are you sure he'll be at home at this time. Don't we have to call him first?" I was procrastinating at a time when I had no second to lose.

He gave me a look as he went to grab his coat and jacket, very much in control of the situation.

"He's always in on Saturday mornings," he said.

I reluctantly joined him at the coat hanger. "So much for being grounded at home!" My laugh sounded weak and put on.

Aboodi sensed my growing nerves and squeezed his gloved hand over mine. "It'll be ok, Ainee. You're not evil. And it's only evil that meets a nasty end."

I smiled weakly but didn't have the heart to remind him that this was, once again, cold and brutal reality we were dealing with.

CHAPTER TWENTY-EIGHT

Saturday
10:10am

The sky was steel grey and the weather was slightly warmer than the past few days. I smelled something disagreeable in the air and was worried that tonight's drama might not be the only storm we would have to deal with.

As we biked towards our grave goal, I kept hoping we wouldn't bump into Mariam on the way. Fortunately, our ride was smooth and uneventful.

The Imam and his wife lived in a little lodge on a small slope in a neighborhood called the Bumping Willow.

We dismounted our bikes and trudged up the slightly steep climb to his doorstep.

His black Range Rover wasn't parked in the driveway.

I raised an eyebrow at Aboodi, my heart thumping in relief as well as disappointment.

"Maybe his wife took it to the shops," Aboodi panted, as he parked his bike on the side of the house and rang the bell.

After three rings, the door swung inwards and the Imam's wife, Layla, looked out, her head wrapped in a towel, and the collar of her robe pulled up to her chin.

"Oh…oh! Children! Why, what a pleasant surprise! *Assalamu alaikum!* Peace be on you!" she gushed, clearly not used to many visitors, especially young ones standing on her doorstep.

"*Wa alaikum assalam* – peace be on you too! Ma'am, is the Imam at home?" Aboodi asked politely, smiling at her through the screen door.

She straightened her turban and pouted her lips. "Aw, dear, I'm afraid he went buffalo hunting with Mikaeel Morrison. Everyone's meat supply was getting low so they thought they would do it a week early and distribute it around. But don't just stand there, come on in! I've got porridge on the stove!"

Aboodi skipped form one foot to the other and looked to me for an answer.

"Thank you, Mrs. Imam." I said sheepishly. "But I'm afraid we should get going. Maybe some other time when he is at home…"

"Nonsense, child!" she shushed me as she unlocked the screen door and swung it open. "Come inside. It must be freezing out there! Where's your Mommy? What have you come to see the Imam for?"

Oh no. I had forgotten what an inquisitive mind she had. Aboodi and I shared a look. But Layla didn't give us a chance to escape.

She practically reached out and grabbed both of us by our sleeves and yanked us indoors. "Do you think I will let you go off like that after coming all this way! Ooh, what an inhuman beast I would be if I let you do that!"

"No...please...we don't mind...we like inhuman beasts..." Aboodi tried hard to resist her tows but failed miserably.

In a few seconds, we found ourselves seated in two hard armchairs with bowls of steaming porridge scalding our thighs, without knowing how we had gotten there.

"So," Layla said, after she had run into her room to change into a blue sweater dress over baggy pants, with a matching *hijaab* and cloak. "What brings you here, my lovelies? Does Mariam know you're here?"

"No." Aboodi said glumly, while trying to shift the big bowl from his left thigh to his right.

"What have you come to see the Imam for then, little darling?" she turned towards me, her hands clasped on her knees, her eyes brimming with flashing question marks.

"Just...stuff." I said, staring into my porridge. It was very thick and lumpy and I was certain something had just moved in there.

"Oh, I am sure, he would be here shortly. He left after morning prayers you know. I'm sure the boys have caught a lot of juicy red buffalo meat haha!"

I grimaced and looked at Aboodi. He seemed to be trying to place the bowl between his legs but apparently got scalded there too. He gritted his teeth and glanced at me, his face red, his eyes streaming.

"Well, shall I get you some juice with that, dears," she asked, inclining her head towards the porridge.

"Yes please," I smiled though my teeth. As she stood up and turned her back to us, Aboodi and I, in one motion, tilted our bowls into the big coniferous potted plant resting between our chairs.

There was a slight sizzling, gurgling noise.

"You don't think the plant will die do you?" I whispered.

"Who cares?" Aboodi nearly barked out. "*I* nearly died. And I hadn't even tasted it! Besides, I think the plant is fake."

Layla returned soon, with two tall glasses of orange juice. Or something that looked like it.

"There you go dears," she exchanged the empty bowls for the glasses of juice.

This is going to be a long day, I thought, not sure if I should be grateful at how slow the minutes were crawling.

It wasn't until noon that we heard the sound of a vehicle pulling into the driveway.

"Ahaaa!" Layla sang out girlishly as she twirled a finger in the air and jumped off her seat. "Yusuf's here!"

"It's about time..." Aboodi grumped, tossing aside the photo album that had been placed forcibly on his reluctant lap for the last hour and a half.

My earlier uneasiness returned in mounting stabs to my heart, as I placed my half empty glass on the wooden floor and turned towards the front door.

"Assalamu alaikum, habeebty," Imam Yusuf's tall and imposing figure darkened the doorway, as he bent to peck his wife's cheek.

"Honey, we have a couple of young visitors waiting to seek your advice!" she sang, giggling and turning towards us.

His black eyes looked over her head and found me, and all I could hear now was the distinct lub-dub of my heart like an approaching train.

"Assalamu alaikum, Yasmine," he said, his lips slanting bemusedly. "Assalamu alaikum, Abdallah, my man! What brings you here today?"

He moved away from the doorway and the pale light from outside found its way in again.

I focused on his unexpected grin and did not find it difficult to convince myself that he didn't appear so frightening after all.

Abdallah stood up and went over to shake the Imam's hand, while I took in the pile of skinned buffalo hide drooping from a rope around his neck.

"Good game today!" he nodded to me in response to my unasked question. "We even got quite a few, puffy Rock Ptarmigans to last the month. Everyone can have partridge for their supper tonight! Tally-ho! *Alhamdulillah*- All praise to God!"

He removed his chain of fresh hide from around his neck and handed it to his wife. "Layla, please clean and quarter them. Insha Allah, I want to deliver them to the Mehmets and the Ebrahims by this evening."

"Just gimme a few minutes, guys," he nodded to Aboodi and me. "I can't concentrate when I'm soaked in grime. I'll have a quick shower and we can sit by the fire and swig a cuppa while we have our little chit-chat."

"He doesn't seem so bad now does he, Ainee?" Aboodi whispered consolingly to me after he had gone. The sound of the tap running and the steady thud of a knife against a chopping block proved that Layla was also out of earshot.

"I dunno, Aboodi," I smiled softly. "The difficult part is yet to come."

We waited for about ten minutes before the Imam returned in a clean white *thope* and with his frizzy black hair and beard still damp from the shower.

"So, what can I do for you two?" he asked, ensconcing himself in a wooden rocker by the fireplace and sipping from a mug of steaming coffee that Aboodi and I had politely declined. "I ran into your Mom on my way back. She was at the mechanics. Car broke down or something while she was shopping. She was worried that you guys were barking each other's heads off at home."

Aboodi and I glanced at each other and I understood that he wanted me to begin speaking.

"Imam," I said, after clearing my throat.

"Mmm?" he looked to me with eyes that seemed surprisingly kinder than ever before. Suddenly I felt that with the topic I was going to present to him, I was wishing for more aggression and belligerence on his part. This heart could never be satisfied, I realized.

"Imam, we came to you to discuss a serious matter and without beating around the bush, I shall straightaway tell you…" I looked at Aboodi.

He tensely nodded at me, urging me to continue.

"-that I'm not Yasmine. I'm Ainee."

There was a silence of about thirty seconds except for the continued thumping emanating from the kitchen.

I watched the Imam's face, waiting for his reaction but he was frowning into his coffee.

"Go on." He said.

I glanced nervously at Aboodi and saw that he too had expected the Imam to jump up shrieking Quranic verses of protection or at the very least look stunned.

But his face just looked impassive and thoughtful.

"I have inhabited Yasmine's body for the last three years," I continued, building up momentum with every passing second that did not include the Imam literally shooting daggers at me. "I didn't mean to. I know it is wrong. But I did it with the best intention at heart. I did it to save her life. But soon after, I dunno, something happened. Both of us clashed or something. That is why she was sick for so long and I had lost my memory up until now. It's like for the last three years neither one of us could achieve total control of her body and both of us were just drifting aimlessly.

Unfortunately, now I am gaining advantage and as I grow stronger, she grows weaker. She doesn't have much time to live. We came to you hoping that you will help me get out of her and spare her life. Will you help us?"

Both Aboodi and I watched the Imam with bated breath.

But all he did was maddeningly continue to sip his coffee, his eyes focused somewhere on the ground.

I looked to Aboodi helplessly and he mirrored my expression. Suddenly, I wanted to get up and scream at him to use every possible hex he knew, no matter how much it ripped me apart, for this dead suspense was agonizingly worse.

Finally, he placed his empty cup on the coffee table and looked at me, his eyes narrowed. "Are you done?" he asked quietly.

"Er…yeah?" I wasn't sure where this was heading.

"Ok," he said, getting up to his feet and towering over us like a giant. I could have sworn Aboodi cowered in his chair too. "Now, get up and get out of my house. I've had enough of nonsense for the day! Out!"

I opened my mouth in disbelief. *Nonsense*?!

"But we are telling you the truth, sir!" Aboodi spoke up in my defence.

"OUT!" the Imam roared. "You and your childish idiosyncrasies! How dare you come all the way to my place to feed me with such garbage? Do you think I cannot figure your lies out? ARE YOU TRYING TO INSULT ME?!"

"But...but...we need your help! Tonight, Yasmine will die! You have *got* to help us!"

"OUT!" he screamed and the chopping sounds in the kitchen stopped too, so Layla could eavesdrop on us.

"Don't try to infuriate me, girl! You don't know who you are playing with. And I am not referring to myself. Making up sinister stories about the unknown is what many kids like to do thanks to the garbled TV shows they watch these days! But it's not funny. Please go home now. And tell your Mom that I'll be bringing her some meat this evening, if the expected snowstorm doesn't start early. I promise I won't say a word of your raucous behaviour if you leave now without a word."

I was still reeling from his unexpected reaction. He had erupted all right, but for the wrong reasons.

"I can't believe this!" I murmured angrily to Aboodi, as we stood outside the Imam's house, hastily putting our gloves on.

"Me neither," Aboodi said, still stunned that we had been thrown out unfairly. "What are we going to do now, Ainee? Tell Mom?"

I shook my head, turning to glare through the front window of the house. I felt a sudden anger towards the Imam and myself too, for not choosing the proper words to make him believe my story.

"It's not like we have a choice," I finally turned away, after throwing my dirtiest, angriest look at the person watching us from inside.

CHAPTER TWENTY-NINE

0100

We reached home an hour before Mariam arrived.

The weather forecast on the local radio station predicted a snowstorm with winds peaking at about 50 km/h after ten pm that evening.

Already it had begun to snow softly, but other than that, it was mostly calm.

"Well, maybe Alisa won't be having her party if there's a snowstorm tonight," Aboodi said, as he flung his cap miserably onto the dining table.

I shook my head moodily. "No, knowing Alisa, she will milk the time for all its worth and have her party till about nine pm. Beyond that is when the storm starts, so she needn't cancel the entire thing."

"Do you feel any different?" he asked me anxiously, as I sat next to him on the three-seater.

I shook my head, looking straight ahead. "Nothing except anger. And disappointment and failure. A huge yawning failure."

"You know, it's weird," he said. "All these big words coming out of a little girl's mouth. Me having to call you by a different name. Funnily, I just realized I had never been close to my kid sister and now after knowing you, I feel terrified at the thought of losing her. Well, several times today I was wondering if this is all a dream and I might wake up tomorrow and find that everything's back to normal."

"Yeah, but define normal." I asked. "Seriously, ever since you guys came to Sand Point, you've not been normal. That ship sailed ages ago, kid. Promise me one thing. Once it's all over and I am no longer with Yasmine, promise me that you and your little colony will move away from here. This is not the right place for you. Go somewhere warmer, somewhere where there is more of your kind…just relocate, please!"

His eyes were wide. "But…"

"No buts, Aboodi," I said, tightly squeezing his big, calloused hands. "Promise me now. Either way, I will be leaving Yasmine. And I don't know what would happen to all of you should Vesta and Zeenon choose to redirect their fury on you. You have got to go. Promise me!"

His lower lip was trembling. "I…I…but will you die too, Ainee?"

"Promise me!"

"I promise!" his voice broke and he turned away from me.

I reached out and pulled him forward in a tight embrace.

He cried into my- his little sister's shoulder, probably wondering if she would be there tomorrow morning for him to cry in relief.

"Don't go, Ainee," he sobbed. "I'm so scared. What will happen to us? What will they do to you?"

I stroked his lean, broad back, mothering him while I tried to keep my thoughts in one place. I didn't want to think of what would happen to me. Right now, there were other lives to save that my own impending doom seemed tiny in proportion.

❄ ❄ ❄

Mariam walked in, her hands piled high with grocery bags.

"A little help?" she said, and Aboodi and I jumped up and ran to her rescue.

"There, have you been good children?" she asked once all the bags had been placed on the dining table.

Aboodi rolled his eyes, trying to act his usual goofy self. "Ma! Stop embarrassing us already!"

She smiled but then extended a worried hand to touch his flushed face. "Are you alright, darling? You look feverish."

He shrugged and turned his back on her, pretending to be involved in the unpacking of groceries.

"He's fine, Mama," I smiled and babbled, "We're just worried about the snowstorm tonight."

"Why, dear?" she asked, frowning, as she opened the fridge to place in a new carton of milk and a container of berry yogurt. "You've never found storms to be alarming before!"

I shrugged too, wondering if this was the time to disclose everything. From Aboodi's stiffening back, I assumed that he was also thinking along the same lines.

"Ma..." I began but stopped abruptly when I saw that Mariam was still unpacking stuff with a look of concentration on her tired, pale face.

"Yes dear," she said, scrutinizing a box of lasagna.

"Nothing," I said instead, smiling sadly, for here was a lovely, down to earth woman I was deluding day in and day out with my foolproof appearance. "I just wondered if you might be hungry. I could set the table?"

"Excellent!" she straightened up and smiled warmly. Her eyes crinkled around the edges and I wondered what it might have been like for this family if I had never intervened in the first place.

❄ ❄ ❄

Lunch was leftover creamy pasta from last night. All of us ate like there was no tomorrow – in my case literally.

Afterwards, Mariam sat back in her recliner, with her eyes closed, and the Quran playing in the background.

Aboodi and I sneaked anxious glances at each other trying to gauge the best moment to deliver the bombshell.

Just when I opened my mouth, Mariam laughed softly, her eyes still shut serenely.

"I'm so glad things are working out between us, as a family. Just when I thought we were goners."

I exhaled empty, pitiful air instead of the words I'd chosen to break Mariam's heart. Aboodi balled his fists in tacit annoyance.

"Mom," he said, hoping to thwart her before she launched herself into full philosophy mode.

She opened her eyes and her expression immediately became animated. "Just last week, when everything was topsy-turvy, I would have never imagined I would be feeling such inner peace as I am feeling now. It's true, "after every hardship comes ease…" God says in Chapter 94 in the Noble Quran." Apparently her son's attempted interlude had fallen on deaf ears.

"Mama," I said, grabbing the ball from Aboodi. "You remember the hallucinations I was having up until a few days ago…"

She sat up in her seat and looked at me. "I know! Alhamdulillah, they're no more right?"

I shook my head. "No, it's not that…in fact it's…"

She snorted and looked from me to Aboodi. "And that Doctor Cardiff made my blood boil with his foolish diagnosis! Epilepsy he said! As if! I knew I did the right thing when I gave him a piece of my mind and walked away from that filthy place!"

"Huh?" I was thrown off balance. "Epilepsy?"

She sniffed and leaned forward to clasp me in a tight hug. "I never told you, hon. But Cardiff's impression was you were suffering from petit mal seizures which usually disappear by the time a child turns twelve. But he was dubious in your case and wanted to carry out numerous tests to rule out the possibility of grand mal seizures occurring later on in life. I think that's pure baloney! I told him so too!"

"Oookaay..." this was getting more and more preposterous and with every second we were drifting away from our original purpose.

"Oh, are you sure you don't have any super powers or anything at all?" Aboodi burst out in desperation and both Mariam and I looked at him in surprise.

"N-no." I said. "It doesn't work like that, Aboodi, I told you so!"

"But she will never understand! And time is running out!" Aboodi was almost crying again.

"What are you guys talking about?" Mariam's face was twisted in between humor and bewilderment.

And then without any warning, I was hit with a splitting headache. It nearly cleaved my head into two and I almost buckled under the wave of utter agony that crashed down on me.

"Ainee! Ainee!" Aboodi's voice floated into my wavelength as if from another dimension.

"*Yasmine!*" Mariam's muffled shriek.

"I...I...don't knowww...I...I...Aaargh!" I staggered into the coffee table, holding my head in my quivering hands.

"Ainee!"

"Yasmine!"

I felt a hand grab mine to steady me, but I looked up and snapped in a voice that was a garbled, distorted version of my original voice and Yasmine's melded together. "*Leave…Me…Alone*!"

I saw through blurred eyes, Mariam shrink back from me, one hand frozen out in front of her, the other pressed to her chest. Aboodi was equally frozen in place behind her and both their eyes were wide as if they had seen a ghost. Or worse.

I panted and snarled, feeling mixed emotions surge up from deep within me, like molten lava churning within a volcano in symphony with the pounding of my head.

"*Not…much…time*!" I grunted and spluttered in anguish, tearing at my throbbing head, my voice still a beastly fusion of my two selves. "*She is…slipping away…it feels…horrible!*"

Aboodi hesitated for a second, but jumped to his senses and grabbed hold of me. "Yasmine! Hang in there!" he screamed, shaking me vigorously.

And as soon as he shouted those words, my spasms receded. My migraine of all migraines ceased to exist, and the breath that puffed out of me was that of a little girl's once again.

"Aboodi!" I sobbed, clinging onto him and shaking in fear and distress.

He rubbed my back until I had gained a more normal semblance and then both of us slowly faced Mariam who was staring at us, as still and white as a marble statue.

"Who are you?" she asked in a high-pitched voice before her eyes rolled back in her head and she dropped heavily to the floor in a dead faint.

CHAPTER THIRTY

0500 hrs

"She's asleep. She hasn't slept well in ages and her body is relishing it now." I whispered as I tucked the quilt under Mariam's chin.

"But she's been out cold for a few hours," Aboodi said, tensely wringing his fingers. "Are you sure we don't need to call a doctor?"

I raised an eyebrow at him, while I stood up from the couch we had lifted Mariam onto after she fell unconscious.

Her eyes were peacefully shut in a deep slumber and her breathing was regular.

"You forget I am more than five hundred years old, kid," I told him. "Do you think I would not have picked up the ways of your folk in that amount of time and would not be wiser than a doctor?"

"And still be unable to free yourself from my sister." Aboodi snorted bitterly.

I chose not to reply him. Every minute that ticked by was increasing the tension between and within us.

Outside, the wind was starting to pick up as well.

I switched the TV on.

"-As opposed to earlier calculations, increasing winds are seen heading toward the East Borough by eight pm tonight," the weatherman was saying. "Residents of Sand Point are requested to restrain from driving after seven pm and to stay indoors and keep their pets and doors and windows in check, as the severity of the storm is rapidly increasing. And moving onto other…"

I switched the TV off and reached for the phone.

Dialing Samiya's number, I waited impatiently for someone to pick up. After about twelve rings, a harried voice wheezed into the phone, "Hullo?"

"Samiya…er…is Samiya there? May I speak to her please? It's Yasmine."

"I'm afraid she's gone to bed, sweetness," said Samiya's mother. "We are busy hauling out the goods from the boot of the car, shoulda done that in the morning, haha – but no point crying over spilt milk anyway, what with this approaching storm…"

"Why is Samiya in bed?" I asked frantically. "It's only five-ish pm!"

"Oh, she's been catching a sore throat, hon," Samiya's mom said. "It got worse this afternoon. Would you like to leave a message? I'll make sure…"

"No thanks," I said hastily, remembering that Samiya had sounded perfectly fine to me that morning. "Thank you! Goodbye, Mrs. Mehmet!"

I slammed the phone down and shook my head.

"Where is she?" Aboodi sat up in his seat opposite Mariam's couch.

"Supposedly in bed," I muttered, rushing to grab my coat. "That is the oldest and the lamest trick in the book. The foolish little girl is willingly falling headfirst into dreadful danger."

"But you can't go out there!" Aboodi stood up. "The storm's just starting and what if you have another fit on the way?"

"I have no other choice!" I argued as I pulled my knit cap over my forehead and draped a muffler around my neck. "I can't let something happen to Samiya! She'll either get stranded out there in the snow or have Vesta pouncing on her before she can squeak, 'blizzard'. This situation is fickle."

"But what about Yasmine?" he asked, and as an afterthought, "What about you?"

I looked him straight in the eye. "Abdallah. I promise you, I will not let your sister go without a fight! I will do everything in my power to save her. Trust me!"

"But we don't have a plan!" He shot back.

And Allah is the best of planners. So, put your trust in Him, said my conscience in the voice of a long-lost loved one.

"Put...put your trust in God," I stammered. "For He is the best of planners."

And ignoring Aboodi's speechless expression, I yanked the front door open and looked to the stormy sky. Allah, I thought. *Allah.*

But I must have had some pride and arrogance and perhaps a lot of the wrong kind of fear in my heart to pronounce the name. I still couldn't get my tongue to say it.

If only I had known then, that uttering the precious, authoritative, unique name of God would have brought instant help in a vibrant flash, I wouldn't have delayed in doing so.

05:30 pm

"Assalamu alaikum dear, oh my! You shouldn't be here! The storm is approaching!" Mrs. Mehmet greeted me in shock. "I don't see Mariam's car. Did you come here all by yourself?"

Samiya lived down the street from us, Aboodi had pointed out, and it took me slightly longer than a usual five-minute walk would have taken me had it been under normal weather conditions.

"I was worried about Samiya," I said curtly, as I brushed past her and stomped into the house. The place did not look familiar at all, for now I was viewing it with almost a hundred percent of my own memory. "Is she up there?" I asked, gesturing towards the winding staircase.

"Yes, but..."Samiya's mother began, but her father showed up from the living room and interrupted, "What's all this about...Oh Yasmine! Didn't see you there, kid! Wait- did you come here all by yourself? In this despicable weather?"

"Yes, Mr. and Mrs. Mehmet." I said sardonically, as I jogged upstairs. "Someone needs to check on their daughter especially when she suddenly develops a weird sore throat!"

The Mehmets glanced at each other for a split second before bolting up the stairs after me.

I stopped at the dimly lit landing, wondering which of the three identical closed doors lead to Samiya's bedroom.

Her mother however, pushed past me and turned the knob on the door to the left, and we stepped into a quiet and dark room, lit only by the star-shaped nightlight on the farthest wall.

"Samiya?" Mrs. Mehmet said hesitatingly, as her hand reached out to flick the light switch on.

The whole room was bathed in light. All of us focused on the bed where a huge lump lay under a pile of blankets, solid and unmoving.

"Oh boy," I breathed.

"Don't tell me…" began her father edgily.

Mrs. Mehmet drew back the covers in one slick movement and both parents gasped at the huddled train of pillows, towels and cushions that occupied the bed instead of Samiya.

"My baby!" her mother screamed and teetered backwards into the waiting arms of her husband.

"Not again! No not again! Not after what happened three years ago!" Mrs. Mehmet wailed, while Mr. Mehmet's stony gaze never left the bed.

A chilly wind whipped through the room and my eyes fell on the window that was left ajar, probably when Samiya had made her stealthy exit.

"Look," I said, turning around to subdue them. "I think I know where she is. At Alisa Mahn's party on 142 Tolstoi Avenue. If we hurry there, we will find her!"

"Alisa Mahn?" her mother asked, struggling to focus her horror filled eyes on me. "But I forbade her from going there! It was to be a mixed party!"

"Mrs. Mehmet, forbidding someone to do something doesn't guarantee they won't do it!" I said. "Now, if we hurry, we'll be able to go there and get back before the storm erupts!" And the word 'storm' carried more meaning than one to me.

Without further ado, the three of us piled into Mr. Mehmet's Volkswagen and set off to Alisa's place.

CHAPTER THIRTY-ONE

0600 hrs

Tolstoi Avenue was at least four kilometres away, and as the Volkswagen sped forth in the increasing gale, I wondered how long ago Samiya had left home for it all depended on if she had already reached safely or not.

I kept my eyes peeled for Samiya's figure, as we passed various shops, houses and landmarks.

However, by the time the vehicle cruised to a halt in front of number 142, there had been no signs of Samiya trudging along the way and I secretly prayed she hadn't been nabbed by Vesta.

"Why, what's this?" Mr. Mehmet exclaimed and I snapped to my senses and pressed my face to the fogged-up window pane.

The Mahn's house was unlit and looked desolate.

"Are you sure you have the right address, Yasmine?" Mr. Mehmet twisted around in his seat to look at me worriedly.

I nodded. There was only one Alisa Mahn in the whole of Sand Point and I had checked and re-checked the directory after copying down her address.

"Wait here," he unbuckled his seat belt and opened the door. An icy gust of wind entered the car.

I unlocked my door and stepped out of the car too, despite Mrs. Mehmet's weak words to constrain me.

I strode up the vacant driveway and looked towards the house. Not only did it look like there had never been a party here, but it was also obvious the inhabitants were not in.

"Mr. Mehmet," I began, reaching his bulky form, when he gave a startled cry and rushed forward to the Mahn's porch.

I narrowed my eyes, trying to spot what he had seen, when Mrs. Mehmet joined me. "Where…where is everyone?"

"Dunno, Mrs. M," I said, moving forward slowly, bracing my heavy and somewhat throbbing legs against the nippy wind and the falling snow.

"Samiya, how could you!" Mr. Mehmet had crouched to the ground and was cradling a limp, silent form, in his arms.

Mrs. Mehmet shrieked from behind me and rushed forward. "Is she…is she…"

"She lied to me Mom!" I heard Samiya's weakened voice ring out. "She left this note tagged to her door. There had never been a party! She and her family are in Vancouver for the weekend!"

I reached the porch and saw Samiya heavily jacketed and steadily sinking into despair. Her face was white and her eyes were swollen from crying, but otherwise she appeared to be perfectly alright.

"Let's get her into the car. We can sort out this tomfoolery once we reach home." Mr. Mehmet rose to his feet, carrying his woebegone daughter in his arms.

I mutely followed suit, grateful that at least one danger had been averted.

"How can we ever thank you, Yasmine?" Mrs. Mehmet sobbed, holding my hand from the front seat. "If you hadn't been so concerned, Samiya would have died of hypothermia or something! May Allah bless you child! You are a true friend and a model child for anyone to have! I wish I had brought up my selfish daughter to be like you! Oh my God, I still can't believe we came so close to losing Samiya for the second time!"

Samiya was seated beside me in the rear seat, her face pressed to the cold window. I squeezed Mrs. Mehmet's hand and smiled in response.

The car pulled in front of my house.

"Get in and stay safe kid," Mr. Mehmet turned around to fix me with a look of admiration and awe. "Tomorrow when the storm passes, your bravery will not go unnoticed. We shall see you in the morning! God bless you and your family for your big hearts!"

"Goodbye, Mr. and Mrs. Mehmet," I said simply. "Get home safe and please don't let Samiya out of your sight! Keep her with you for the night!"

"Will do, my love," Mrs. Mehmet embraced me warmly, before I climbed out of the car slowly, as my knees suddenly felt sore. "You are also my daughter. Remember that! We shall never forget your unselfishness. See you tomorrow, Insha Allah! *Assalamu alaikum!*"

I looked at Samiya, for she had slowly turned towards me.

Forgive me, her eyes pleaded. *Forgive me...my friend.*

I nodded, happy that one storm had passed and feeling that tonight was the night I would cancel all grudges sitting in my account.

"Wa alaikum asalam," Peace be upon you too, I responded for the first time in my life, loving the way my tongue rolled around the greeting of peace.

CHAPTER THIRTY-TWO

0630pm

There was a black Range Rover sitting in our driveway.

Feeling apprehensive about the Imam's presence in our house, I blinked away the stinging bits of snow that hurled across my eyes and face and trudged forebodingly to our front door.

The strange pain was slowly sliding up my legs and splaying across my lower abdomen, as I knocked stalwartly on our front door, a stranger to my own house.

"Come in," echoed a muffled voice from inside.

I pushed the door open and stepped over the threshold, wondering what lay in store for me beyond the hallway.

"*Assalamu alaikum*," greeted the Imam, as I stepped into the living room, and I saw the three of them- Aboodi and the Imam on the couch and Mariam propped up by the crackling fireplace – turn their heads toward the doorway to look at me.

"*Wa alaikum asalam,*" I said warily, as I slowly removed my cap and shrugged off my coat onto the nearest chair.

My eyes took in Mariam's peaked face and scared, distrustful eyes and the Imam's vigilant, brooding stare. Aboodi, I guessed, looked the friendliest, with his anxious and jittery expression.

"Sit down, Ainee," the Imam said and I raised an eyebrow in response. Mariam, I noticed, twitched at the name I was called.

"Yes, I know who you are," the Imam explained, nodding civilly at me. "I apologize for not believing you at first, but you must understand that the revelation you gave me was most peculiar and startling!"

"What made you change your mind?" I asked him, while I slowly and painfully lowered myself into a chair opposite the Imam and Aboodi.

"When you were leaving my house, you looked back towards the window," The Imam recounted. "And I saw your eyes blaze with a fury I have never seen before. Your eyes literally burned a bright red!"

Aboodi pursed his lips, disturbed, while I merely nodded as if I'd known this all along. "I...didn't realize it then but yeah I guess you're right. I felt the heat emanating from them. Aboodi, you got your wish, bud, I do have super-vision after all!"

I gave a weak laugh directed at Aboodi, but it was Mariam who suddenly sprang up and screeched out at me,

"Who are you, you impostor? I want my daughter back! *I want my baby back!*"

"Relax, sister!" the Imam reprimanded her, and she reluctantly sat down again, her eyes still boring into my -not Yasmine's this time- soul and cursing me.

"So, after that staggering phenomenon, I hurriedly sought out my books and combed every bit of information ever written about the *unseen world*. That's the only reason I took this long to come here. That and this awful weather."

I looked into his eyes with hope spreading tinglingly across every nerve in my body. "Can you help free me? Can you help save Yasmine's life?"

"I will try. But everything is in Allah's hands," he said.

I shivered and nodded, as the pain arched across my midriff.

The Imam cleared his throat. "Normally we begin with a question regarding your faith and why you entered the victim's body. Then we say the *Azan* or the call to prayer. And as we progress, I have to warn you that it doesn't get easy for you."

I nodded solemnly. "I understand. But right now, all I'm concerned about is Yasmine's life." I coughed and the pain stabbed me in the chest.

"Liar!" Mariam snarled, her veins standing out in her forehead. "How can you be concerned about my Yasmine if you possessed her in the first place? How can you...oh my God, this is so unreal!"

"Abdallah!" the Imam craned his neck towards Aboodi, and raised his voice, "Please take your mother upstairs! If she cannot endure what she is witnessing, then I'm afraid she will not be permitted to hang around here!"

"No! No!" Mariam said, her voice sounding deranged, as she held out her hands in protest. "I'll stay, I'll be quiet! I just want to see that creature die before my eyes! Every single day I was being deceived by her! I thought it was my daughter each time I fed her, slept by her, cried for her and showed affection to her! And all the time it was that evil...!"

"Mrs. Ebrahim! Final warning!" the Imam glared.

She finally shut up and sat down but the effect of her words continued to stab me.

The Imam shook his head and once again looked at me.

"Are you a follower of the religion of one God and a believer of the fact that Prophet Muhammed, peace be upon him, is the final messenger of God?"

I trembled slightly, staring into his intense eyes. "I know this but I'm not sure if I do believe," I whispered.

"What's stopping you from believing?" he asked gently, leaning forward and looking at me intently.

"I have done many sins. Very major ones. How can I believe if God would not choose to accept me?"

"God is known as *Ar- Rahman* and *Ar- Raheem*, *Al – Wadood* and *Al- Ghaffar!* His mercy exceeds his anger. Verily, all of us go about the wrong way talking about God's wrath when his love for His own creation exceeds the love of a mother to her child, more than seventy times! If you truly repent for any sin that you have committed, what makes you think He won't accept it?"

I gulped. "Because I have followed the Devil for centuries. I feel that my heart has blackened beyond repair, because when I heard the truth, I shunned it afterwards. I...I don't know how I can turn it all around."

The Imam smiled softly, and I felt that all this time I had been barking up the wrong tree and running away from the one person who could have helped me from the beginning.

"If you say your heart is blackened, Ainee, you wouldn't be seated here worrying about an innocent girl's life over your own. And you wouldn't have come to me for help this morning."

"Yeah, that..." I glanced at Aboodi. "I was in two minds actually."

"Say: "O my Servants who have transgressed against their souls! Despair not of the Mercy of God: for God forgives all sins: for He is Oft-Forgiving, Most Merciful." The Imam recited. " Surah Al Zumar (The Troops), verse fifty-three. How can you deny God's mercies when it has been stated and sealed in the Noble Quran?"

"But..." I faltered.

"And say: Work; so Allah will see your work and (so will) His Apostle and the believers; and you shall be brought back to the Knower of the unseen and the seen, then He will inform you of what you did." He continued. "Surah Taubah (Repentance), verse 105. Now how can you continue to do evil once you realize that He sees all that you do and you will eventually return to Him?"

"But..."

"What you have done in the past remains in the past, but you have to move into the future with a new goal in mind! With a strong resolve to do good!" he urged.

"I want to, believe me!" I said, my chest throbbing and pulsing with pain.

"Ainee," he said sternly. "I cannot extricate you, if you don't help me. You are stuck because of your own confused emotions. Just focus. Believe in what you think is right. Your heart knows the truth. You, I and all of creation were crafted by the One. All of us were born with the truth in our hearts, but it's our vain desires that lead us away from the light."

I was sobbing. "There is no good," I echoed Vesta's words, the words I had been brought up with for eons.

"Of course there is, love," he said. "There is good in everything! Every good is from Allah and every evil is from *Shaitan*. It's up to us to choose. So, what is your choice?"

"I...can't! I...can't" I cried, clutching my chest and quaking with grief. "I just...can't!"

He leaned back, his face portraying the disappointment he was feeling inside. The third person I had betrayed in my life.

"Then you leave me with no choice, Ainee," he declared, sorrowfully. "Unless you repent and reform, you will not move forward, for you will still be a devil. And the devil shuns away from one thing always..."

CHAPTER THIRTY-THREE

I wept and wept while I was seated askew on my chair, clutching my aching chest, my rejected dreams and my broken promises.

The Imam towered above me, and I watched through bleary eyes, Aboodi shrink back in dread and Mariam lean forward expectantly from her corner of the room.

"Are you sure about this, Ainee?" He asked me with distress melting the coal of his eyes.

I barely managed to nod. Yes, I wanted Yasmine to survive, above my own survival. Three years of my possessing her would all crumble to dust otherwise. Putting his hands up to his ears, the Imam boomed in a beautiful and stentorian voice, rippling with authority and might: "Allahu Akbar, Allahu Akbar!"

I reflexively convulsed and jerked forward in my seat.

"Allahu Akbar! Allahu akbar! Ashadu Allah ilaha illallah..." *God is great, I bear witness that there is no God but Allah...*

My throat constricted and my head nearly imploded with a fierce pain that sliced through it.

"Ashadu anna Muhammadur Rasoolullah..." *I bear witness that Muhammad is the Messenger of Allah.*

"Ainee...!" Aboodi's voice floated in from far, far away...a life line -one that I felt would not help me even if I attempted to grasp it.

" Ashadu anna Muhammadur Rasoolullah..."

Yasmine! I felt her. I felt her slip away even as I sank to the floor in violent spasms and screams.

"My baby, my baby! Oh, what's happening to her! HELP HER, PLEASE! PLEASE!" Mariam's voice now.

Yasmine! I screamed and she sighed in response- tired, spent and defeated. I opened my mouth to call out for help, but the paralysis had just about brushed my vocal cords. Only my eyes bulged out, begging, pleading and wrestling for assistance.

"Hayyalas salah!" *Come to prayer.*

"Ainee!" I felt Aboodi's racking sobs and presence by my twitching side.

"Hayyalas salah..."

And then a new sensation on top of the excruciating ordeal I was already going through – I felt a thin, snake like rope slither into my nose and form a familiar loop in between my nostrils.

Vesta! Oh no! I panicked as I realized Yasmine must be within a second of drifting away because I was being pulled back into Vesta's grasp.

Help! I pleaded with my eyes once again, but my own vision skated away from the living room and showed me images of my past. Cities, Oceans, Forests, Zeenon, Al Barak, Vesta, Yasmine – these images of my past swam in front of me paying a last tribute to the one who nurtured them.

"Hayyalal Falah! Hayyalal Falah..." *Come to victory, come to victory.*

The rope around my nostrils sealed and hardened, invisible yet definite.

"Yasmine! Yasmine! Oh my God, she's slipping away! Oh, help her, Allah, help her!" My body was being shaken and clutched and squeezed. I heard cries and screams ringing in the background.

A vision of Al Barak swam in front of my eyes.

"Allah created men and jinn to worship Him. What other purpose in life do we have? At the end of the day all our achievements are turned to dust. Only our deeds remain, for they are our train fare to Paradise. So, start collecting them. You still have good in you, Ainee. Don't waste it! Don't waste it!"

And then my eyes opened. Not just my visual senses, but my entire being felt like it burst open and at the same time succumbed to the truth of life.

"I bear witness to the fact that there is no God but Allah. And, Muhammad is the final messenger of Allah!" I said, I exclaimed, I screamed.

There was instant silence. It was as if the earth stopped moving. Time stood still as every particle in the air stopped in its tracks.

And the *touch of frost* was lifted.

Like a blanket being raised, portion by portion, I felt myself float out of the little girl's still body, free and wraith like until I was hovering above her, watching the scene from the ceiling.

The Imam and Aboodi were bending over a stricken Mariam who was cradling a lifeless child in her lap. Mariam's cries wrung my heart and I breathlessly scanned little Yasmine's face, for the first time in three years, without the help of a mirror.

"She's gone, she's gone, oh my baby! She's gone too! Like Sa'eed, she's left me!" Mariam wept like she was being killed slowly and mercilessly, and I could feel every ounce of her sorrow.

"*Inna lillahi wa inna ilayhi rajioon,*" The Imam whispered, kneeling across from Mariam. "To him we belong and to him we shall return. This life is temporary, sister Mariam. We are all born into this world not knowing how we will die. The time of death is jotted down by an angel while the child is still in the mother's womb. It's *Qadrullah* – the Divine Decree. This life is ours to live and the choice is always there between good and evil. But in the end we all have to die and return to Him. We have to accept it." He was crying too.

"She is so small and tiny. So weak! And all this time she had been fighting that monster inside her! How can I bear this? How can a mother bear to hold her dead child in her arms and realize she had been sick for so long without anyone knowing it! How can I bear this, Imam, you tell me!"

"With Imaan, sister," he said, wiping his eyes. "With faith! Truly, God tests those who are patient. Little Yasmine will be there in heaven *Insha Allah* waiting to welcome you with open arms. She will beseech Allah to admit you into paradise. She is your confirmed ticket to *Jannah* because of the incomparable grief you are going through now. Have faith and courage sister! Have faith, have faith."

Mariam hugged her only son to her while she embraced her daughter as if she would never let go.

All of them were sobbing and I watched helplessly and with sadness I had never felt in my life, ever before.

This must have been how the thousands of mothers felt when they lost their daughters, I realized. Each time I took them away, this was the grief they were going through. It is not easy to lose a child and it's even more difficult to lose one while she was alive only a while ago in your arms.

"Mommy…" a little voice like the promise of spring or a beautiful pony prancing into sight, crept through the sobs.

"Mom!" Aboodi said, his face white, and his eyes almost popping out of their sockets. "Mom…she…she…"

And suddenly Yasmine opened her eyes, her clear hazel eyes, sharp and un-streaked with sapphire as had been the case when I was with her.

All of us jolted as if we were struck by lightning.

"YASMINE?" Mariam screeched, her mouth wide in disbelief.

"*Subhanallah*! Glory be to God!" the Imam gasped.

"YAYYYYYY!" Aboodi pumped his fist in the air.

"Mommy, what's going on? What happened?" Yasmine, in her pure little voice with her sweet little smile, sat up and looked around her in wonder.

It was without a doubt, even to the humans watching, that 'Ainee' was not in her anymore. The child's entire form had changed. She looked fresh and whole, and very much alive.

"La ilaha illallah!" the Imam shook his head while Mariam was drenched with a fresh attack of tears as she hugged Yasmine and bathed her with kisses all over her head, face and hands.

"It's good to have you back, lil sis!" Aboodi clapped her back, his eyes raining down tears of intense relief.

"Welcome back, darling! Oh Allah, all praise be to you for sparing my little angel! Alhamdulillah!" Mariam cried, as she pressed her cheek to Yasmine's and rocked to and fro.

"But where did I go?" Yasmine asked curiously.

"To a place you shall never go to ever again, with Allah's help!" Mariam shuddered.

"'And we will surely test you with some fear, hunger and shortages of property, people and produce. But give good tidings to the steadfast. Those who, when a calamity befalls them say: We belong to Allah and to Him we return. Upon these are prayers from their Lord and mercy and these are the rightly-guided ones.'" the Imam quoted joyously. "And also, ' After every hardship comes ease.'"

Mariam nodded, biting her lip to quell more tears from flowing.

"But Imam," Aboodi looked around him. "Where's Ainee now?"

Mariam took a sharp intake of breath but didn't say anything.

The Imam frowned thoughtfully. "She uttered the Shahadah in the nick of time. That should have liberated her. She should be free now, Abdallah. She did the right thing. She saved both Yasmine's and her life. May Allah make her one of the righteous. Aameen!"

I saw Aboodi's face stiffen and his eyes darken. "But she will be in terrible danger now! Her Master will torture her!"

"Aboodi, you got your sister back, what more could you ask for? Will you stop saying that wretched name in my house, please! She has brought us enough of trouble!" Mariam said.

"May Allah protect her from now on, Abdallah," the Imam said, stroking the teenager on the arm soothingly. "She has submitted now and she wears the shield of honour. She knows not to trespass anymore. She has repented for her past. There is nothing more we can do for her. She knows she cannot consort with us anymore."

Aboodi nodded but didn't look too happy.

"Come on, everyone, let's all pray and thank God for bringing our little angel back to us!" Mariam said giddily, as she shakily climbed to her feet still clasping Yasmine's hand tightly.

The little troop left the living room and I watched them with a poignant stab to my heart, feeling that my story here had finally ended.

CHAPTER THIRTY-FOUR.

As I turned around to blink away from the house, another surprise greeted me.

"Assalamu alaikum!" said a deep and joyful voice and I saw hordes of shimmering shapes hover outside the window.

The voice was so familiar and it sent goose bumps up my arms.

"Wa alaikum asalam?" I whispered warily, as the shapes took form.

"Why do you look as if you fear us?" the voice said again and for the second time that night I was seized with a spasm to my heart, as I saw the face of my beloved spring into focus.

"Al Barak?" I said, immediately blinking out and reappearing outside the house.

The storm had just begun with fleeting snow and ripping winds, but it had no impact whatsoever on my immaterial form and distracted mind.

"I haven't seen you in ages!" I said, shock and inexplicable joy coursing through me. "I thought you despised me and had forgotten me! How are you here? Oh, how are you doing???"

He smiled. He hadn't changed much in nearly half a century when we had last seen each other in the clearing in the woods, so long ago, and yet so much like yesterday.

"I never forgot you, Ainee." He said. The way he said my name sent my pulse racing. "I always hoped and prayed that God would guide you. We, my brothers and sisters would always remember you in our *Duas - prayers*."

"But where have you been all these years? Why didn't you contact me?" I looked around at the army of friendly faces smiling at me and I felt so much at home at this precise moment.

"Up until today when you made your declaration of faith, we didn't have anything to do with you." Al Barak looked sober. "You were still one of them, the devils, and all we could do was pray for you. Allah gives guidance to those he wishes to give guidance to, because He knows what's in their hearts. If you were not meant to be one of the guided, because of what was in your heart, then there would have been nothing we could have done for you."

I bit my lips and just stared at his noble face. He smiled and turned away abashedly.

"It was you, wasn't it?" I asked, recalling the vision of him I had seen in my final moments. "That little speech about a train fare to paradise and the goodness inside of me…that wasn't a memory…it was you whispering it to me just then!"

He nodded. "Like I said, we were always with you. When we thought we were about to lose you forever, we had to try one last time."

"Welcome to peace, sister!" two women stepped forward and embraced me, followed by more women. I was trying my best not to break down in tears at the sure signs of Allah's mercy that were descending upon me at this blessed moment.

Once everyone had warmly welcomed me into their fold, Al Barak came close yet stopped at a respectable distance. "I have a question to ask you," he said, looking down. "I have waited all these years hoping and wishing for this moment, but only tonight, after your testimony of faith, did it seem possible that my dream may come true."

I waited, my heart pounding in my ears. "Yes?" I breathed. I also noticed out of the corner of my eyes, a few of his companions were waiting for my reaction to his words.

"Insha Allah, with Allah's will, I wish to ask for your hand in marriage…"

"What?!" I was rendered speechless.

He cleared his throat and blushed. "This has been my dream for so long. You always were special, Ainee, 'my eyes'. I am so glad you shed the mottled outer skin that was shielding and ruining your vibrant inner beauty. Now you are pure and whole, knowledgeable and caring, and I wouldn't have any other woman for a wife. You have gone through the test of a lifetime and finally emerged as a brave and noble warrior. So please consider my humble request."

Tears of joy and rapture shone in my eyes and he must have understood what I felt. The group closest to him chorused with shouts of triumph and I was just opening my mouth to present him with the renowned answer, when the forgotten loop around my nose tweaked and I was pulled away from my happy surroundings and into my familiar nightmare.

❄ ❄ ❄

"Why, hello, muffin pie, good to see you again!" Vesta said, her illusionary beauty appalling me, as she sashayed out of the mouth of the cave in Tillman's Gorge.

I blinked and looked around, feeling highly disoriented. The wind was ferociously whipping through the trees and echoing plaintively in my ears, as the white haze of snow lashed across my eyes.

My ears were still ringing with the laughter of Al Barak's clan and the moving question from Al Barak's lips, that I found it surreal to be glaring at the darkness and dreariness of this place.

"You lost, Vesta!" I said, as she stopped within a few feet of me, sneering. "Yasmine lives, and Samiya is safe. So why don't you just retire and get a nice, deserted little bungalow in the Himalayas?"

"Tsk , tsk," she shook her head coyly. "As long as you're still bound to me, I have not lost, mongrel." To prove her point, she swivelled her fist and twirled her slender fingers as if she were slowly drawing on an invisible cord, and inevitably, my head jerked forward ever so slightly.

"You have been very naughty, Slave," she sang in a teasing voice, her purplish eyes wide with madness. "And now you have to pay for it."

Without warning, she yanked, and I tumbled to my knees at her feet.

"Bow to me, slave," she intoned proudly.

"I...will...not!" I pulled my head back and tried to resist, but she continued to yank on the invisible lead, pulling my head further down.

"Bow to your one supreme leader!" she droned, her eyes flashing, her head towering like a fifteen-foot giant.

"My one...and only... supreme leader is..." I struggled against the pain of trying to defy her commands. "Is...God Himself!"

She let go and I fell flat on my face.

"You pathetic maggot!" she screamed. "You shall die! Yes! And die slowly! We'll see how you scream for mercy from your Allah, when Zeenon gets here!"

She flexed her fingers and I felt myself slowly transform into a Rottweiler against my bidding.

As my form altered, I felt a change in the wind as thousands of figures glinted into view. Also, as I gradually turned solid, I fully felt the harshness of the blizzard and the coldness of the snow coat my senses.

"Aaah, so we meet again, Mongrel!" Zeenon smiled as he floated towards me, his evil followers at his tail. "How I have missed you through the centuries! I almost envied Vesta her perfect punch bag! Greetings to you too, Vesta!"

Vesta glided forward, tall and majestic. "Greetings, Lord Zeenon. I have kept your prize for you, my Noble Master. Please, I only ask for a small favour in return."

"Ask and it shall be granted, my obedient one!" Zeenon smiled and inclined his head.

Vesta flashed her cruel eyes at me. "When you're done with her, please allow me to make use of her corpse. I want to tarnish it beyond recognition for all the grief she has given me!"

I shivered and I hoped it was because of the cold, for I didn't want her evil words to wreck my new-found inner strength.

O Allah, my mind whispered, as I raised my eyes up to the sky. *I ask for your mercy and not for my life to be saved. Only for your mercy and forgiveness, O Allah! For if I were to die now, I want to be raised up with the status of a believer and a martyr. Please accept my humble prayer, O Merciful Lord of the helpless!*

"Finished?" Zeenon smiled mockingly, while his associates threw back their heads and laughed loudly.

You may kill this body but never my soul, Zeenon, I said to him in my mind. *My soul has already found salvation and there's nothing you can do to harm it.*

"We'll see now, shall we?" he replied, raising his eyebrow.

He raised his arm and flung something invisible at me.

It pierced me like a bolt of lightning that sent innumerable shock waves splintering through every nerve in my body.

I let out an involuntary gasp and Vesta clapped her hands in glee.

"Care for some more?" Zeenon asked me, his smile hardening, as he lifted his arm again and shot two more invisible lightning bolts.

I leapt out of what I assumed to be the path of one bolt, but got singed by the other. This time, a low howl escaped my throat and Zeenon's army circled over me chanting, "Die! Die! Die! Die!"

"I am going to enjoy this little treat!" Zeenon roared and his people cheered.

One after the other, lightning bolts rained down on me and I leapt and hopped and yelped and scrambled within the constricted little circle formed by Zeenon's followers around me.

"Cry, dog! Cry!" Vesta shrieked in laughter. "Lemme hear you grovel!"

I clamped my mouth shut, forcing myself to think of happy moments: Yasmine alive and well, Al Barak thinking of me all these years...

CHAPTER THIRTY-FIVE

"This-"said Zeenon, breaking into my thoughts, as he flung bomb after bomb at my writhing body, "Is what you get for switching allegiances and turning your back on your people!"

"So why don't you treat that despicable weasel, Vesta, also in the same way, you shameless, cowardly creature!" shouted a strong voice.

By then I was nearly spent, with third degree burns all over my fur and face, but I raised my head to see scores of Al Barak's forces confront my oppressor.

"Aaah, Al Barak!" said Zeenon in his slippery voice, not noticing Vesta suddenly cower behind a rock in fear. "Are you here to witness the grand finale? Have you come to say goodbye to your sweetheart?"

"Let her go, Zeenon!" Al Barak growled. "She is not your enemy here. The One you are actually waging war with, will show you what pain's like on the day of Reckoning. For you can keep trying but you will never overpower Him!"

Zeenon laughed and his forces snarled at Al Barak's troop. "Always the pessimist aren't you, my man?" he said. "You always speak of submission and guarding one's gaze, refraining from pleasures of the flesh…seriously, you should have died of boredom a long time ago."

"Do you honestly think you will not taste the Fire?"

"What? When we are made of fire? Surely you jest! How can we be harmed, silly child!"

"That's a legendary saying of your kind, Zeenon!" Al Barak argued. "That's an easy excuse for you to avoid the truth! You think if God created you, he can't raise you from the dead and hand out your sentence accordingly?"

"I grow weary of your insistent babbling!" Zeenon yawned. "What are you even here for, Barak?"

"Set Ainee free."

"Or what?" Zeenon lazily challenged.

"We shall fight, every last man and woman in my army, to win her into our community." Al Barak said gravely.

"What?" Zeenon snorted. "Look at your puny caravan! Mine is nearly three times its size! Are you blind, boy? This creature's life is not worth the mass wipe-out of your people! Go, while you still have the chance. Find another mate! There must be thousands out there worth more than this gribble!"

"You may have a strong army," Al Barak narrowed his eyes, and the muscles in his arms rippled. "But our faith is stronger! That is enough for me! And Ainee is mine. I will fight for her, till my death!"

His people applauded and raised their fists in the air, signalling loyalty to their leader and their faith.

"Very well, then," Zeenon turned towards his entourage and gave a signal. Every last one of them bounded to the ground in the form of husky battle hounds, yipping and snarling with zest.

Al Barak nodded to his team and as one, they transformed into a mixture of wolves, greyhounds and various other predatory creatures.

"What did he mean by calling you despicable Vesta! What have you done?" Amidst the developing foray, Zeenon frowned towards the crouching Vesta.

"N...nothing ma...my Lord," she tried to smile and stand up, but he transfixed her with his piercing gaze and seemed to read her mind.

"Hmm..." he said, after a few seconds had elapsed, fury distorting his features. "I will deal with you later!"

"Come on, Ainee, get up and change quickly, before you pass out!" said an earnest voice into my ears and I groggily looked up into the shining face of a young woman from Al Barak's clan. "Let's get you to safety! You might die!"

With great difficulty, I hauled myself to my wounded feet and limped towards a large rock that looked like it would shelter me from the biting cold and the rampant snow.

"Can you switch now?" she asked me. "The witch seems too preoccupied in controlling your transitions anymore."

I forced my mind to stay awake and concentrate. Slowly and painstakingly, I felt my pains recede as my paws, legs and stomach dwindled into my natural form, and my chest, shoulders and head followed suit.

❄ ❄ ❄

I closed my eyes and leaned my head against the girl's shoulders, every last bit of my body echoing the screams of the dog's body in pain.

"Rest awhile until you gain your strength, Ainee." She said. "I'll be here with you."

But I couldn't rest, not with the ruckus unfurling outside.

Snarls and barks; roars and bellows mixed with the howling and the rushing of the nipping wind and lashing snow.

The battle was reminiscent of Persepolis, only now, I was the object both sides were fighting for.

"I can't let our people die like this!" I protested to the young woman. It felt so good to use the term 'our people' for once referring to the side of integrity. "This is cold-blooded murder!"

"Al Barak will not let them oppress you, Ainee," she replied. "He will fight until justice is served!"

"But I won't allow him and everyone else to die for me! I cannot bear to think of it!"

I rose to the air and struggled to view the scene through the haze of the brutal snowstorm.

And then I made out animals ripping at each other's throats, rearing up on their hind feet or rolling and barking savagely at one another.

"Why can't he just recite some special words of the Quran like he did before?" I asked, pained at the bloodshed accumulating below.

"Because that will just send the devils away and they'll only come back again," my comrade explained. "This time, both parties want to end it once and for all."

I spotted, towards a cliff, two animals rearing and striking each other, with a vengeance that was visible even through the flogging of ice and snow, and audible over the sounds of battle.

"Come on," I urged my friend, and both of us zipped towards the cliffs.

You shall meet your wretched end, Barak, a sleek, sly looking panther, as black as ink, growled.

If mine is wretched, then what will yours be, I wonder? A regal grey wolf grunted back.

The panther leapt on the wolf and tried to scratch his eyes out, but the wolf was quick. He raised his hind paws and thrust a kick into the panther's stomach, sending the latter somersaulting head over heels towards the edge of the cliff.

I watched with bated breath as the fight continued.

"Ainee, look!" The girl pointed towards the west.

I strained my eyes and made out the vague shape of a floating figure dancing haphazardly and waving her arms around in the swirl of frost and snow.

"It's Vesta!" I said. "She's gone crazy!"

Both of us blinked towards the figure, just in time to hear her sing, *"Now you've gone my beautiful child…gone from me…gone forever…no more can we share our dreams, our sorrows, our love…for you have left me standing here, alone…forever!"*

Her eyes were blank and her lips chanted the same song over and over, each time the tonelessness in it escalating.

"Ainee…?" my friend said quizzically, but I watched in dread, as Vesta brandished her arms above her head and…flicked.

A noise as low and ominous as a rumble of thunder shook the already bustling air and increased in intensity. I watched, stunned in a daze of déjà vu as the hills around us came alive.

Segment by segment, piece by piece, snow and rocks started crashing down in tons, as with a groan, the hills began to collapse.

"WARN THEM!" I screamed and my dutiful young friend didn't waste a single second.

I watched Vesta crumple to the ground in fits of laughter, as her body changed from old hag to young woman, then to a prairie dog and back again, in quick, erratic flashes as the tumble of snow bringing unimaginable mayhem, swallowed her up in its wake.

I wheeled around and rushed against the wind, flying low and shouting out warnings: "Avalanche! Avalanche! Headed this way! Take cover! Take cover!"

Every creature whipped its head around even as I was issuing out the warning, for the quaking ground and the approaching roar was growing too loud to ignore.

Those who had the sense to quickly change into wisps of fire and rise into the air, managed to narrowly escape, but the majority of pitiful black creatures from Zeenon's tribe were crushed under the relentless force.

Eager to get the better of their wrath, they had lapsed in their judgment by waiting until the final moment to escape and had thus risked their lives.

I rushed over to the cliff where the personal war between the two leaders raged on.

Matted with blood and splattered with deep and ugly gashes, both panther and wolf were still not giving in to one another.

Surrender, Zeenon! Before you go to your grave a villain! Al Barak uttered a low, menacing growl in his throat. His left eye was swollen shut and his nose was bleeding heavily.

Over my dead body! Zeenon scowled.

"Avalanche!" I screamed.

Al Barak jerked in my direction and then looked over the panther's head.

The avalanche had increased in mass and momentum and was headed like a juggernaut towards the edge of the cliff.

Zeenon whipped around, snarled and pounced on Al Barak.

If I go, I'm taking you down with me! He hissed and pushed the wolf in the chest, with all his strength.

"Noooo!" I screamed in horror as I watched the helpless wolf topple over the edge of the precipice and disappear into the abyss below.

CHAPTER THIRTY-SIX

The snow slide menacingly approached Zeenon, and I saw him gulp and scream ,"I don't want to die! I believe in God! I believe! I believe…"

But the last of his futile screams were crushed mercilessly, as the titanic mass rolled over the cliff and thundered into the river below.

I was still grappling with my shock, when an icy ribbon of wind weaved through me and brought with it a glimmer of hope.

Al Barak's people flocked around, once again in their natural states.

"Where's our *Amir*?" they all asked me. "Where's Al Barak?"

"Watch," I smiled and the slight curve in the air in front of us quivered and filled out into the familiar and glorious figure of the leader we all loved and were in awe of.

The crowd cheered and sang praises to their Lord, while Al Barak shouted in triumph, "Ainee is a free woman! Her days of slavery have ended! The Evil has been wiped out! All Praise be to Allah for saving an innocent soul, and for guiding all of us! Alhamdulillah!"

There was a huge uproar that even outdid the snapping and moaning of the treacherous winds. It continued to puff and gnaw at us, but to me the storm had finally, after a long and bitter three hundred years, ended.

"Yes!" I said suddenly, in the midst of all the cheering and celebrations. Al Barak looked towards me questioningly.

"Yes?" he asked.

"I never had the opportunity to answer your important question," I explained, and now it was I who looked down at my feet in bashfulness. "My answer is, yes!"

I slowly glanced up into his eyes to observe his reaction.

His face lit up in that beautiful, dazzling smile of his and I realized it was well worth all my struggles I had ever endured in my entire life to see this smile reserved especially for me.

Surely after every hardship comes ease...

EPILOGUE

August 12th, 2011
Long Beach, California
Late afternoon

It was a typical summer day in Southern California with the temperature reaching a high of twenty-three degrees that balmy afternoon.

My husband and I were lazing around in the shade of a clump of trees in a modest sized community park, watching the people come and go, unaware of our presence.

Our little children, Sulaiman, Abdar Rahman and Yasmina were frolicking around, and we watched them vigilantly to make sure they didn't playfully steal the human children's toys to use as their own.

"I daresay our little Aboodi takes after you, my Ainee," Al Barak teased me as we watched our third-born pick up oranges fallen at the foot of a reedy tree, and turn them invisible so he could leisurely disembowel them.

"Since when do I eat road kill?" I joked.

"I was referring to your little knack of playing around the borders of our plane and theirs," he winked at me.

I shook my head. "Now look who's breaking the rules and uncovering the past! I can't even pass by an innocent Rottweiler when you quickly blink us all out of the area like we'll all catch rabies from it! Shame on you, Al Barak!"

He smiled but a serious look stole over his face. "I guess I do over react at times…but it's just that I still can't get over the fact that I could've lost you! You were this close to slipping away!"

I stared vacantly at a passing couple and their young daughter. "Well, if Allah wills something, no one can stop Him from carrying it out."

"And to this day I thank Him for sparing your life! There wasn't a day that went by when you were under Vesta's control, that I didn't think or worry about you! And now look at us today! Subahanallah! It's amazing how Allah's plans all work out for the best!"

"Yeah I guess it was destined for me to go through all that suffering in order to achieve what I have right now," I said.

He shook his head. "Whatever wrong you did was your own choosing, for there is always a choice presented to you at the beginning. But what matters is that after you do a wrong deed, you realize the folly of your actions and repent for them. That's what marks your destiny and directs you to achieve your goal."

I smiled. My husband could get so philosophical at times but I also realized that I loved him all the more for it.

"I'm just glad we left that horrible, isolated snow-choked place," I said, shuddering. "I'm sure Yasmine's folks and their friends relocated too. That place holds such awful memories for everyone. I don't see why anyone should continue staying there after going through what they went through!"

"I'm sure they left, Ainee," Al Barak whispered and squeezed my hand.

"Yeah, but I wish we had just gone back one last time to check up on them," I muttered knowing what his reply would be.

"Ah, Ainee," he said right on cue. "How many times do I have to remind you…"

"'…that we should not intermingle with them or try to meddle in their affairs!'" I mimicked him. "I know, I know! I'm just saying is al!"

He grunted good naturedly. "I think it's time we dropped the subject. We are breaching our promise to one another. So please, let's just zip it at that!"

I sighed and looked away. The park was littered with many children and their happy parents, and I was happy to say I was one with them.

"It's time we left," Al Barak said presently, stroking my arm, hoping to soften the after effects of our petty argument.

I leaned my head against his shoulder and looked into his face and smiled. We could never stay miffed at each other for too long. That was the beauty of our relationship.

"Come on children," he called out, and our kids scampered over to us, giggling and bubbling with mischief.

"Now what have you been up to?" I asked, as I kissed Sulaiman and Yasmina on their heads.

"Aboodi is trying to tickle that little girl over there!" Yasmina gurgled in glee.

I followed her pointing finger and saw my irrepressible youngest son reaching out from behind a park bench to flip the hair of a little girl seated serenely with a book on her lap.

"Aboodi! Come over here at once!" I called, as I left my older two in my husband's company and dashed half a kilometre to where my son was about to commit his naughty deed.

"Aboodi!" I chided him. "How many times have Daddy and I told you to never, EVER try to make contact one of them! It's too dangerous and could land us in way too much of trouble!"

My little boy turned to me and the cheekiness in his eyes faded. He withdrew his hand and sulkily blinked away from the scene to join the rest of our family under the oak tree.

I turned towards the little girl, whose back was to me, and sighed in relief, for she had not felt a thing nor heard a word that was exchanged between my son and I.

Her flyaway brown hair waved gently in the breeze and she was so engrossed in her book that I smiled and made to part from the scene.

"Ayna? Ayna! Let's go home, honey! It's getting closer to supper time!"

The name caught me off guard and I turned towards the source of the voice.

A slender, young woman, her hair hidden under a beautiful floral-patterned scarf and a matching burgundy pinafore dress was sauntering towards the park bench.

"Honey, Daddy has some work to catch up on as well, before Uncle Aboodi, Aunt Reem and baby Hamza come for supper. Let's go now, shall we?"

"I wish Myesha and Mina were coming too, so I'll have someone to play with!" the little girl sulked.

The mother sat beside her daughter and put an arm around her shoulders. "We'll have the twins over next weekend, Insha Allah, when Auntie Samiya is able to get off her hospital shift, all right? It isn't easy for a paediatrician to just up and leave whenever she wants to. You know that, don't you? Besides San Francisco isn't far away. We get to see them more often than your Uncle Aboodi in Texas. Cheer up, little heart, baby Hamza is adorable! You'll love him! " She leaned her forehead to her daughter's and smiled mischievously into her eyes. "Also, Grandma is bringing over your favourite pecan-topped, creamy chocolate cake for dessert!"

The little girl giggled, closed her book and jumped off the park bench.

"Alright, Mommy!" she sang, as she skipped across the park, with her mother slowly following in her footsteps.

A sob choked in my throat as I watched the beautiful, petite mother pause and smile lovingly after her little girl, her lips parted over her surprisingly attractive misshapen teeth. It was as if two of her front teeth had never reached maturity.

"*Assalamu Alaikum*, Yasmine," I said softly, scared that she might hear me but also hoping that she would.

Maybe it was instinct, or maybe she did hear a silent whisper in the breeze, for Yasmine stopped and turned around. She stared curiously at the empty park bench, her eyes passing right through me.

She bit her lips and screwed her beautiful hazel eyes, trying to discern something that wasn't there.

"Honey, are you coming!" called a young man's voice and she shook her head as if to rouse herself from a dream, or perhaps a memory.

"Coming!" she called back and turned away, skipping towards the young man just like her daughter had done a few seconds ago.

When she reached him, she turned one last time and looked longingly towards me again. And I wasn't sure if I had imagined a ghost of a smile light up her face, but from then onwards whenever I reflected on this particular scene, I liked to believe that Yasmine had replied to me with *salam* in her heart.

AUTHOR INFO

S. Hafreth was born in the UAE and is currently living in Australia. Coming from and Islamic background, S. Hafreth felt that there were very few books out there (and none when she was growing up), representing Muslims in an everyday environment, doing normal everyday things people did and depicting their beliefs through everyday actions, as opposed to how the media portrayed them. Always an avid reader, cushioned around the works of Enid Blyton, then Christopher Pike, Bryce Courtenay, Jodi Picoult and Margaret Atwood, her pen revolved around a mixture of these authors' genres but nothing held long enough to result in a satisfactory novel. Then in 2011 she stumbled upon an FB page that published creative Islamic poetry and prose, combining the beauty of the written word with spirituality sans the preaching effect. Through that page she discovered other blossoming writers and somewhere in the midst of it all, a story was born, one of mystery, suspense, faith in hardship, and of course frost.

Her interests include reading, especially when she is on a writing hiatus, and writing, after all that reading has hit the roof with inspiration. She also likes to travel, spend time with her husband and two kids and cook (not bake, and you'll find funny stories on her baking disaster, plus more, if you visit the writer's page she co-admins on Facebook, where her true writing journey began, Islamic inspiring Words - IiWord

ALSO BY LBL

Charlotte & Daisy

A novel by
Amanda Huntley

True Talent

The First Mistake

T.R. Earnhart

THE UPWORLD

Lindsey S. Frantz

CPSIA information can be obtained
at www.ICGtesting.com
Printed in the USA
BVHW041636080622
639033BV00007B/64